The chance of a lifetime

The man told them that at the end of the month the winning number would be drawn on the CBS football pregame show, the one hosted by James Brown. It would be like one of those jackpot lottery drawings you saw all the time on television.

"You've got about the same odds as winning a lottery," the man said. "But good luck anyway."

Nate had taken his ticket home and put it in the trophy case with the Brady ball and hadn't taken it out until the day of the drawing, watching with his parents and Abby as James Brown called out the winning numbers, one after another.

Every one of them the numbers on Nate's ticket.

They stopped dancing around and hugging and screaming only when Nate's mom told them to hush so they could hear the representative from SportStuff say that the winning numbers belonged to a thirteen-year-old from western Massachusetts by the name of Nate Brodie, that a boy who was now the most famous thirteen-year-old in America would get a chance on Thanksgiving night to make the throw of a lifetime.

The man from SportStuff said, "A million-dollar throw from a one-in-a-million kid."

James Brown had said, "Hope he's a quarterback."

And Nate said to the television, "I am."

MIKE LUPICA

MILLION-DOLLAR DOLLAR THROW

PUFFIN BOOKS
An Imprint of Penguin Group (USA) Inc.

PUFFIN BOOKS
Published by the Penguin Group
Penguin Young Readers Group, 345 Hudson Street, New York, New York 10014, U.S.A.
Penguin Group (Canada), 90 Eglinton Avenue East, Suite 700, Toronto, Ontario, Canada M4P 2Y3
(a division of Pearson Penguin Canada Inc.)
Penguin Books Ltd, 80 Strand, London WC2R 0RL, England
Penguin Ireland, 25 St Stephen's Green, Dublin 2, Ireland (a division of Penguin Books Ltd)
Penguin Group (Australia), 250 Camberwell Road, Camberwell, Victoria 3124, Australia
(a division of Pearson Australia Group Pty Ltd)
Penguin Books India Pvt Ltd, 11 Community Centre, Panchsheel Park, New Delhi - 110 017, India
Penguin Group (NZ), 67 Apollo Drive, Rosedale, North Shore 0632, New Zealand
(a division of Pearson New Zealand Ltd.)
Penguin Books (South Africa) (Pty) Ltd, 24 Sturdee Avenue,
Rosebank, Johannesburg 2196, South Africa

Penguin Books Ltd, Registered Offices: 80 Strand, London WC2R 0RL, England

First published in the United States of America by Philomel Books,
a division of Penguin Young Readers Group, 2009
Published by Puffin Books, a division of Penguin Young Readers Group, 2010

7 9 10 8

Copyright © Mike Lupica, 2009
All rights reserved

THE LIBRARY OF CONGRESS HAS CATALOGED THE PHILOMEL BOOKS EDITION AS FOLLOWS:
Lupica, Mike. Million-dollar throw / Mike Lupica. p. cm.
Summary: Eighth-grade star quarterback Nate Brodie's family is feeling the stress
of the troubled economy, and Nate is frantic because his best friend Abby is going blind,
so when he gets a chance to win a million dollars if he can complete a pass during the halftime
of a New England Patriots game, he is nearly overwhelmed by the pressure to succeed.
ISBN 978-0-399-24626-5 (hc)
[1. Football—Fiction. 2. Contests—Fiction. 3. Blind—Fiction. 4. People with disabilities—Fiction.
5. Friendship—Fiction. 6. Family life—Massachusetts—Fiction. 7. Massachusetts—Fiction.]
I. Title. PZ7.L97914Mi 2009 [Fic]—dc22 2008047529

Puffin Books ISBN 978-0-14- 241558-0

Design by Richard Amari.
Text set in Oranda

Printed in the United States of America

For my wife, Taylor, and my children, Christopher, Alex, Zach and Hannah Grace: They have given me a world beyond anything I imagined. And become my best friends along the way.

Acknowledgments

Dr. David Hunter, Dept. of Ophthamology, Children's Hospital Boston, Harvard Medical School. Dr. Stephen Rose, Chief Research Officer, Foundation Fighting Blindness. The great Terry Hanratty, who once lit up college football Saturdays at Notre Dame. Billy Goldman, of Highland Park, Illinois. Esther Newberg. Bene and Lee Lupica, who still make me look for the best in myself. And, of course, Michael Green: I'm just sayin'.

CHAPTER 1

This was always the best of it for Nate Brodie, when he felt the slap of the ball in his hands and began to back away from the center, when he felt as if he could see the whole field, and football made perfect sense to him.

Sometimes when you were thirteen nothing seemed to make sense, and the world came at you faster and trickier than flying objects in a video game.

It was never like that for him in football.

Never.

Nate had been having more and more trouble figuring out his world lately, especially with everything that had been happening to his family. School was school—he tried hard, but there were times he just felt lost, in search of answers that wouldn't come.

And no matter how hard he tried, how hard he *could* try, he was never going to make sense out of what was happening to his friend Abby.

But on a Saturday morning like this, underneath all the sun and blue sky, with the guys in the line already into their blocks and Nate feeling as if he had all day to throw the ball—feeling that weird calm he always felt in the pocket—he had all the answers.

Football was like this for Nate Brodie.

As he scanned the field now, he recognized one of those answers he instinctively knew. Pete Mullaney, his favorite receiver, was about to break into the clear. Once he did that, Nate knew Pete was going to run all day.

When it was just Nate and Pete and some of the other guys on the team playing touch football in the empty lot next to Nate's house, they called this play "Hutchins-and-Go." One day Nate had told Pete to fake toward the Hutchins' house, the one on the other side of the lot, fake like he was running a sideline pattern in that direction, and then, as soon as the guy covering him bit, Pete was supposed to plant his outside foot and spin and take off down the sidelines.

The play had just always been called Hutchins-and-Go after that.

Nate watched as Pete sold his fake now, sold it like he was selling candy, didn't rush, even turned and looked back for the ball. That was when the defensive back on him committed, turned, and looked for the ball himself.

Only Pete was gone.

And the ball wasn't coming, at least not yet.

Now it was just a question of what kind of throw Nate wanted to make. Because with the kind of arm he had—his buds and teammates always called him "Brady," knowing that Tom Brady was Nate's all-time favorite player—there were a couple of ways he could go. Nate could put a lot of air beneath the ball, really hang it up there and let Pete use those jets of his to run under it. Or Nate could gun one right now, throw one of those dead spirals that was the same as one of his football fastballs, put so much sting and hurt at the end of the pass that Pete sometimes said he wished he was allowed to wear a catcher's mitt.

Nate decided to put this one way up there.

Moon shot.

He rolled to his right now, feeling pressure coming from his left, a right-handed quarterback's blind side, without actually seeing it. But just to make sure, to know exactly how much time he had, he shot a quick look over his shoulder and saw that the Hollins Hills' nose tackle had cleared Malcolm Burnley, Nate's center and the best blocker Valley had, on an outside route and was coming hard, thinking he might have a shot at getting his first sack of the day.

Nate knew he didn't.

In no hurry, Nate kept moving toward the sideline, toward the Valley bench, almost feeling as if he were floating. Having cleared the pocket completely, a nice patch of open green waited for him a few yards in front of Coach Rivers.

He stopped now, planting, making sure to square his shoulders so he didn't drop his arm angle and sidearm the ball, setting himself on his back foot, carrying the ball high. The throwing mechanics that Coach said you pretty much had to be born with.

And he let the ball rip.

Knowing that the cornerback who had been covering Pete was never going to catch up with him and that the Hollins Hills safety had no chance of getting over to the sideline in time.

He watched the ball like it was on a string, like one of those perfect casts his dad used to make across the water when the two of them still had time to go fishing together, before his dad began working all the time.

He hoped his mom was getting this on the video recorder that was on its last legs and had been for a while, because his dad— working a double shift on Saturdays now—wasn't here to see it in person.

The ball came down into Pete Mullaney's hands, Pete in perfect stride, just crossing the Hollins Hills 10-yard line.

Pete pressed the ball to the front of his white uniform with those sure hands of his and crossed the goal line. Then he turned and just tossed the ball to the referee, because if you played on a-team with Nate Brodie, if he was the one throwing you the ball, you knew enough not to do some kind of crazy touchdown dance afterward.

You could be happy, just not happy enough to show the other team up.

Nate was running down the sideline now, almost as fast as Pete just had. All the things that were confusing about his thirteen-year-old life lately—the things that made him sad and just plain mad once he got away from a football field—Nate had left them all in his dust.

By the time Nate got to Pete, the little wide receiver was on the Valley sideline, waiting for him with his arms stretched wide. Nate, taller than Pete by a whole helmet, grabbed him, picked him up, put him down just as quickly, as much celebration as he was going to allow himself, mostly because there was still some game left to play.

Pete said, "That throw was legit."

"You always say that," Nate said.

"No, Brady, this time I really mean it. That throw was, like, *righteous*."

Nate laughed now, couldn't help it. "I had the wind behind me."

Pete Mullaney shook his head, smiling from behind his face mask. "Dude," he said, "as far as I can tell, your arm is pretty much where the wind *starts*."

Nate ran over to Coach Rivers then, to get the play. Coach wanted them to run on the conversion. Then he ran back on the field and told his teammates he was faking to LaDell and then taking it in himself, on a roll to his left.

Nobody touched him. Valley was up 22–7. They all knew the game was over, even with the clock showing two minutes, straight up, left.

He and Pete ran off the field together, knowing that the forty-yarder they'd just hooked up on had put this one in the books.

When Nate got back to the bench, Coach Rivers gave him a simple handshake.

"A Brady throw all the way," he said.

"I wish," Nate said.

"I'm serious," Coach said. "Biggest throw of the season."

For now, Nate thought.

For now.

CHAPTER 2

It had started out almost as a dare from Abby.

They were at the mall a couple of months ago, right after the school year had started, Nate there with Abby and his mom on what they all knew was a very big day for him. He had turned thirteen just the week before, but that wasn't the big news.

The big news was that after more than a year of saving up birthday money from relatives, Christmas money, and allowance money, Nate finally had earned enough for his share of the football.

And not just any football.

This was the signed Tom Brady ball that he'd spotted in the trophy case at SportStuff the summer after he'd finished sixth grade.

Nate was smart enough about collectibles to know that this wasn't the only signed football from Brady in the world. He knew from asking the man at the store that this particular ball was part of a new "limited edition" from Brady, and it came with a certificate of authenticity.

"How many are in the limited edition?" Nate had asked the

man at the store, and the man, smiling, had said, "Enough for us to charge what we're charging."

Five hundred dollars, plus tax.

Nate read about money in sports all the time, read about the money the top athletes, including Tom Brady, were making. Some of them, like LeBron and A-Rod and Tiger Woods, earned up there in the hundreds of millions. But since he'd had his eye on this ball, it wasn't their salaries that seemed like the biggest number in sports.

It was just the cost of this one signed football.

When he told his mom and dad about it, they told him that if he was willing to save up, if it was the present he wanted the most, they would pay half. It would be a way of earning something off the field the way he always had on it. Or earning a good grade in school, which they always told him should mean even more to him, because they all knew school came harder to him.

And his parents had stayed with the promise even though things were different now in their house than they had been when he'd finished sixth grade. *Everything* was different now that his dad was working two jobs after losing the only one Nate had ever known him to have, at the big commercial real estate company he used to work for.

His mom had gone back to work, too.

"You don't have to do this," Nate had said to his dad one day. "I can wait and save up the whole five hundred myself, even if it does take longer."

"Actually, I have to do this more than ever."

"I don't understand," Nate said.

"A promise is a promise," his dad had said, "even if it's one you make only to yourself."

For all Nate knew, his parents had been saving up for the Brady ball right along with him, waiting for the day when there was finally enough money in the top drawer of his desk to make the trip to SportStuff he'd been dreaming about for what seemed like forever.

SportStuff had become one of the biggest sporting goods chains in New England. They didn't just sell the usual "stuff," sneakers and spikes and jerseys and T-shirts, basketballs and hockey sticks and gloves and bats and balls. The thing that set SportStuff apart was a section of every store known as "The Hall"—as in Hall of Fame. That's where the coolest stuff in the place really was.

The collectibles, all the signed balls and jerseys and memorabilia, all authentic. Signed sneakers, some of them looking as big as a bathtub to Nate. Baseball and football cards, some real old, some *real* valuable, perfectly preserved behind or under glass.

But nothing was more valuable, at least to Nate's eyes, than the Brady ball.

Tom Brady had been Nate's guy from the time Nate first started playing organized football in the fourth grade and started watching pro football games with his dad on Sunday afternoons. In fact, the first game Nate really remembered watching—or caring about—was Brady's first Super Bowl against the St. Louis Rams. That was the day he'd driven the Patriots down the field at the end of the game even though he was basically a rookie. Brady had driven them down the field against a Rams team Nate knew from his dad was a two-touchdown favorite, got them close enough to the end zone that Adam Vinatieri could do something he would do again a few years later for the Patriots: kick a field goal to win the Super Bowl as time ran out.

Vinatieri got to make that end-of-game kick again because Brady drove the Patriots down the field *again* in Super Bowl XXXVIII, this time against the Carolina Panthers.

The first time, though, was the one Nate knew he would always remember best. He didn't understand everything that was happening in the game, didn't understand everything the announcers were saying, no matter how patient his dad had been explaining things. Nate just understood in his heart that there was magic in the room that night, not just because he was getting to stay up later than he ever had to watch the ending of a game, but because he was *sharing* this night and this ending and this one amazing football game with his dad.

Ever since there had been the same kind of magic for Nate every time he watched Brady play quarterback for the Patriots. There was that kind of magic even after Brady hurt his knee and lost that time from the prime of his career. The two of them had shared something important with that first Super Bowl, even if Tom Brady had never known it.

"Anybody can do it when the pressure's not on," his dad would say when Brady had turned into Two-Minute Tom again. "It's when you're *under* pressure, when the whole world's looking at you and your teammates are looking *to* you, that's the measure of a champion in sports."

Now, that day in September at SportStuff, Nate was going to hand over his money and take home the Brady ball and put it in the case his mom had bought for him on his birthday, the one that was waiting for him back in his room on his desk.

He had called the store right before they made the drive over, just to make sure that he hadn't miscalculated on the tax. His mom was carrying the envelope with the money in it in her purse. And there the ball was when they got to the store, right where it always was, directly behind the cash register in The Hall, high up on a shelf between a Kevin Garnett basketball and a bat signed by both David Ortiz and Manny Ramirez of the Red Sox.

"I'd like to buy the Brady ball, please," Nate said, pointing up at it.

The man said, "Sorry, kid, not for sale."

But he must've seen what happened to Nate then, Nate actually feeling his legs buckle, as if somebody had brought him down from behind in the open field. So right away the man said, "Sorry. Bad joke."

Abby, standing next to Nate, said, "Just a *bad* joke? You're being way too easy on yourself, Mister."

The man laughed. "Who's she, your bodyguard?"

And Nate had said, "Something like that. Just a lot tougher."

It was when the ball was in Nate's hands, a ball that Brady had to have handled if only long enough to sign it with a Sharpie, that Abby had noticed the entry forms.

The man was still counting out the money at the time. While he did, Abby got right up on top of the little poster on the counter and started reading out loud. That was how she and Nate found out that SportStuff was sponsoring a promotion called "The SportStuff Million-Dollar Throw."

The winner of the contest was going to get the chance to make one throw—from thirty yards away, through a twenty-inch hole—at halftime of the Patriots' Thanksgiving night game against the Colts.

Whoever made the throw would be handed a check for one million dollars.

The poster showed a picture of the Patriots' home stadium, Gillette Stadium. At midfield, they'd set up a billboard with "SportStuff" written in gigantic letters across it.

Only the place in the middle where the two words should have connected was empty. That's where somebody would try to put the million-dollar throw on Thanksgiving night.

Abby was right on top of the poster now, squinting, somehow managing to read the contest rules.

Nate said, "What do you have to do, go through some kind of tournament like you do in Pass, Punt and Kick?"

"Nope," she said.

Then to the man she said, "Borrow a pen, please?"

"What are you doing?" Nate said.

"Getting a pen for you to sign up with."

"Right."

Abby looked at him, smiling her best smile, and said, "You could make a throw like that with your eyes closed, Brady."

Always the eyes with her. Her favorite expression, one she used all the time, was about the eyes being the window to the soul. Nate wasn't sure he totally got that one, but he tried to act like he did, even used it himself sometimes, never wanting Abby to think he was a step slow keeping up with her in what he called "the smart world."

"I'm not signing up," he said.

"Yeah, Brady, you are," she said. "It says right here that all you have to do to qualify is make a purchase of more than five hundred dollars, which I believe you've just done. And be thirteen or older. There it is, game, set, match."

The man behind the counter said, "But if you're under the age of eighteen, you need a signature from a parent."

Nate's mom said, "He's got one of those right here."

She signed. Nate signed. The man told them that at the end of the month the winning number would be drawn on the CBS football pregame show, the one hosted by James Brown. It would be like one of those jackpot lottery drawings you saw all the time on television.

"You've got about the same odds as winning a lottery," the man said. "But good luck anyway."

Nate had taken his ticket home and put it in the trophy case with the Brady ball and hadn't taken it out until the day of the drawing, watching with his parents and Abby as James Brown called out the winning numbers, one after another.

Every one of them the numbers on Nate's ticket.

They stopped dancing around and hugging and screaming only when Nate's mom told them to hush so they could hear the representative from SportStuff say that the winning numbers belonged to a thirteen-year-old from western Massachusetts by the name of Nate Brodie, that a boy who was now the most famous thirteen-year-old in America would get a chance on Thanksgiving night to make the throw of a lifetime.

The man from SportStuff said, "A million-dollar throw from a one-in-a-million kid."

James Brown had said, "Hope he's a quarterback."

And Nate said to the television, "I am."

CHAPTER 3

Suddenly Nate was famous, at least as famous as a thirteen-year-old from Valley, Massachusetts, could be.

Now, in Nate's living room, they had just watched a story about him on SportsCenter with some clips from the Hollins Hills game, including the throw he'd made down the sideline to Pete.

"SportsCenter," Pete said as they watched the show in Nate's living room. "That is as fresh as it gets."

"Fresh to death," Malcolm Burnley said.

LaDell, the Patriots' tailback, said, "Look at you, throwing a ball to Mullaney on national *TV*." He shook his head and said, "That's what I call putting your *man* suit on."

Abby, sitting between Malcom and LaDell on the couch, just sighed. "You guys talk about SportsCenter like it's church."

"Church with highlights," Nate said.

"How did I end up being the lucky girl included in this boys club?" Abby said.

"You're not just in the club," Pete said, "you're practically a member of the team. Except you never have to get hit."

"Or end up at the bottom of the pile and the guy on top of you has breath that smells like feet," Malcolm said.

"Okay," Abby said, "that's a little more information than I need."

For all the other things that had happened since Nate won the lottery—the big feature about Nate in the *Valley Dispatch*, the one in the *Boston Globe*, another on the NVC station out of Springfield, Massachusetts—the SportsCenter they'd just watched was the best of it.

By far.

It didn't matter what age you were or what sport you played, being on SportsCenter was like having every sports fan in America going to your Facebook page. It was why Nate had invited Abby and some of the guys to come over and watch with him after practice on Monday.

Now the guys were getting ready to leave. Valley was a small enough town that Pete and Malcolm and LaDell would all be riding their bikes home. Abby wasn't going anywhere, she would be staying for dinner, even though Nate hadn't made any big announcement about that. Even if he had, none of the guys would have said anything about it. They were all cool with the fact that Abby wasn't just a part of their crew, she was Nate's best bud.

"A dude who happens to be a girl," Malcolm had said one time. "An almost-perfect combination."

As soon as the words were out of his mouth, Abby had pinched him, because that was her signature move when she thought one of them had stepped out of line. "What do you mean by *almost* a perfect combination, big boy?"

They didn't have TiVo anymore because things like that were too expensive in the Brodie house these days, now that just about everything—with the exception of the Brady ball— seemed too expensive. But they still had their old-fashioned VCR that had "4-head" written over the place where you inserted the tape. So Sue Brodie had taped SportsCenter, and when the guys were gone, Nate and Abby and his mom watched it one more time.

When they finished, his mom got up and rewound the tape so it would be cued up to the exact right place when Nate's dad came home from work later. Then she said she needed to finish getting dinner ready.

Nate thought her eyes looked watery, as if she was getting ready to cry about something.

"You okay, Mom?"

"Better than okay, actually."

"You sure?"

She put a finger to one of her eyes and said, "You mean these? Happy tears."

"I never get that one," Nate said. "How can you be happy and sad at the same time?"

"You'll understand when you're older."

"I'm not sure I want to," Nate said.

"I just want you to enjoy every single moment of this," his mom said.

"I just wish it was Thanksgiving night already," Nate said.

"It will be here soon enough," she said. "You just promise me you're going to enjoy the journey."

"Promise."

Then his mom said, "And in this house a promise is a promise," and headed off to the kitchen.

Abby had moved over to a chair next to the window and was drawing in her sketchbook, even though she knew she only had a few minutes before they were going to sit down and eat.

Abby McCall was good at just about everything. She was the smartest kid and the prettiest girl in the eighth grade in Valley— not that Nate would ever say the pretty part out loud, to her or to anyone else. But she was best at drawing—it didn't matter whether she was working with a pencil in the sketchbook she always seemed to have with her, or working with colors, color combinations that only she seemed to be able to see, on one of the canvases back in her room.

Because more than anything, Abby McCall thought of herself as an artist.

And these days she was painting even more than ever. Nate watched her now, not saying anything, seeing the concentration on her face, as if she were the one taking a team down the field with less than two minutes to go.

As if she were the one on the clock.

"You gonna let me see that?" Nate said.

"When I'm done," she said, not looking up, her right hand flying all over the page as if it had a mind of its own.

"Your mom's right, you know," she said.

"About what?"

"About you enjoying all this and not putting too much pressure on yourself."

"C'mon, Abs," he said. "How can I not? I mean, if I ever make the throw, which I have no chance of actually making, that money would change everything for my mom and dad. Starting with the fact that they wouldn't have to work so hard. My dad might go back to having one job instead of two."

"I heard that," Sue Brodie yelled from the kitchen. "You can worry about money when you're a dad someday. We'll handle it around here until then."

Abby closed her sketchbook, walked over to where Nate was sitting on the couch, and pinched him hard on his left—nonthrowing—arm. "I thought we had a deal," she said. "Did we not have a deal?"

"We did."

"And the deal, as I recall, went something like this: This isn't a job for you. It's an adventure."

Nate grinned. "I'm almost positive you stole that from somebody."

"You do *not* want to tangle with me on this," Abby said. "You're the one who's always telling me that the very best part of sports is how it can make a new memory for you practically every day. And right now you've got a memory going that will last both of us our whole lives, whether you make the throw or not."

She called out to Nate's mom, asked how much time there was before dinner, was told five minutes, and went back to her chair. She opened her sketchbook back up and put her face so close to the paper Nate thought her nose was going to touch as she studied her work. "Even though you *are* going to make that throw," she added.

"How can you be so sure?"

"You know me," Abby said. "I see things nobody else does."

They had a rule, Nate and Abby:

He never looked in her sketchbook without permission.

But he was allowed to *ask* to see something. Which is what he did now, the two of them sitting out on the Brodies' small screened-in back porch after dinner, Nate asking to see what she'd drawn when they'd been inside watching SportsCenter.

"Okay," she said, opening up the book, leafing through pages of drawings Nate knew he'd probably never see, the ones that were for her eyes only. "But I want you to know it's nothing you're going to want to slap a frame on, Brady, it's just a fun thing."

It was an amazing fun thing.

Nate knew how fast she'd done it, knew it should have looked like the first draft of one of his papers for school, with scratch-outs and corrections all over the page. Only it didn't look that way at all. Somehow, just using her pencil, it was like she'd taken a picture of what the room had looked like with all of them sitting there in front of the television.

She'd imagined it as if she were on the side, in front of the picture window. So you saw Malcolm's face from the side, and LaDell's, and Pete's. You saw Nate more clearly, and his mom. Somehow you felt how intensely they'd all been focused on the set, which is where Abby had some fun, having a football flying out of it, as if it were on its way through the window and out of the room.

"A *fun* thing?" Nate said. "Abs, this is awesome. *Awesomely* awesome."

"It's okay, Mr. Art Critic," she said. "I could have done better with the picture inside the screen, so I took the easy way out, with the flying football."

"Yeah, that's obviously going to take your grade *way* down."

She leaned over, as if a pinch were coming, making Nate flinch. And making both of them laugh. "You know as much about art as you do needlepoint," she said. "Or pedicures."

"I know enough to know what's good and what isn't," he said. "And I know you're as tough on yourself after you draw as I am on myself after a game. Even if we've won." Nate pointed to her book and said, "How come you're not in the picture?"

She closed it up and said, "You know me. I like to be invisible and let everybody else tell the story. Wait till you see what I'm going to come up with the night you make the bazillion-dollar throw."

He smiled at her. But then, smiling at Abby McCall, at the things she said and the things she drew and the way she was, felt as natural to Nate as throwing a football. They had always gone to school together, always lived a block away from each other. Nate couldn't remember a time when they hadn't been best friends. Not Nate's "girl" friend. Just best friend.

Mostly she was just Abby.

Nate's mom called her a force of nature.

She must have felt him staring at her as she looked out into the backyard with night falling, Nate wondering, as always, what she really saw.

"What?" she said.

"Nothing."

"Don't nothing me."

"I was just thinking."

She turned and smiled back at him. "Always a good thing, at least until it starts to give you a headache."

"I was just thinking," he said, "how great it would be if we could just keep talking about me making that throw, and being excited about me making the throw, but me never actually having to go there and make it."

"We've already been over this a hundred times. You're going. I'm going with you."

Nate said, "Where else would you be?"

"Exactly," she said. "That night I'll be up in the stands, cheering you on as you put the ball through the silly hole and we all live happily ever after."

Nate didn't say anything to that because he never knew what to say when Abby said something like that. It was almost completely quiet now in the back of the house. Nothing from inside the house, where Nate's mom was reading. No traffic sounds from out front.

"You have to see me do it," Nate said.

"Don't worry," she said. "I will."

"But you said . . ."

"Forget what I said, things haven't been so bad lately."

"You never say things are bad."

"This is another thing we've gone over, Brady, about twelve thousand times. Things aren't good or bad with me. They just are what they are."

"I don't want them to be what they are."

Abby said, "This isn't one of your games. You can't control everything because you're the best player on the field." She smiled again. "The boy with the golden arm."

"Doesn't mean I can't want to," Nate said.

"And guess what?" Abby said. "When I hear the crowd that night after you make your throw, I'll be able to see everything perfectly."

They both knew she was lying.

Because the truth about Abby McCall was that she was going blind.

CHAPTER 4

Nate remembered the first time he had known there was a problem with Abby's eyes. It was a year ago, and they'd decided to go to the movies on a Saturday afternoon in the summer even though most of the guys had gone over to the public pool at Coppo Park.

It was the movie about Kit Kittredge, All-American Girl, and wasn't one Nate would have gone to see himself, even on a bet. But Abby never complained when he wanted to see one of his movies—Abby called them all the same thing, *War of the Exploding Car-Chasing Aliens*—so Nate went along with her, just to keep her company.

It was something he knew he could never possibly explain to his buds or even to Abby herself. But for Nate, it wasn't just sitting back in the pocket where he felt the best.

It was pretty much in any room that Abby was in.

So they went to the movies. And Nate didn't have a clue at the time, because she hadn't said anything, that she'd started having a terrible time with her night vision. And that she'd already begun to lose most of her peripheral vision.

When Nate found out that part later, he'd said to her, "You

can have some of mine." Meaning his peripheral vision, his ability to see the field in front of him like it was in that wide letterbox format he watched movies in. Nate couldn't just see the whole field, he felt like he could see *behind* him sometimes, when a would-be tackler thought he had a clear shot at him from that blind side to his left.

Blind side.

It was what all sides were becoming for Abby, like walls closing in on her.

He knew all about the disease called retinitis pigmentosa now. Just not then. All he knew that day was that when they were inside the theater, a few minutes late, there was this night scene that made it hard for even Nate's eyes to adjust to the dark. And when they were halfway down the side aisle looking for seats, Abby just froze.

Nate didn't know right away. He had spotted a couple of seats and said, "Right there, Abs."

Only she wasn't behind him.

She was about twenty feet back up the aisle, not moving.

"I can't," she whispered loudly, and for a second Nate stupidly thought she just didn't want to sit in the middle seats he'd managed to find.

"Okay," he whispered back. "We can move closer if you want."

Then Abby finished her thought.

"I can't *see*," she said.

Nate walked back up the aisle to her, still not getting it, saying, "I can't see too good, either."

And in this small voice, not sounding anything like herself, she said, "No. I can't see anything."

Then the movie went back to daylight and it was like a light switch had been thrown in the theater, and they'd made their way to their seats, and just like that she was back to being Abby. "Well," she said, "that was certainly weird."

"Well, *yeah*," Nate said.

Abby poked him and said, "No, I meant weird that *you* were *my* guide for a change."

It was her way of making things all right, saying it was no big deal, joking that she'd suffered the eye version of one of Nate's famous brain cramps in school. And Nate went right along with her, because he always did.

Only now he knew that was the real start of it, everything that was happening to her, and there was nothing anybody could do to stop it.

It was the beginning of everything, and it had forced Nate to learn about how eyes really worked—or didn't work—about rods and cones and colors.

About how Abby's world was on its way to being as dark as a movie theater.

That was the summer when Abby realized it was more than her having a problem going from dark to light, more than bumping into things at night, more than having trouble sitting at her window and staring at the stars, one of her favorite things her whole life.

He knew now that the loss of night vision and peripheral vision were just two of her symptoms, knew that the cones closest to the center of her eyes were already making her sense of color go haywire. Abby herself had told him that, explaining why her paintings looked the way they did, explaining that if they both looked at the same rainbow and then she painted it, the colors would look completely different than they had to Nate, as though she were living on the other side of the rainbow.

"It's why it's going to be all right, Brady, you wait and see," she'd said. "Sometimes I feel like I'm painting better than I ever have."

In those moments Nate would want to scream at her, even though he never would, that she wasn't going to be able to paint anything once the keyhole shut completely.

That's the way he saw things inside his head when he imagined the way the world was starting to look to Abby McCall.

He saw them through an old-fashioned keyhole.

Nate had looked up retinitis pigmentosa on the Internet after Abby had finally told him the truth about what was wrong with her eyes. He'd found a "Fighting Blindness" website. And right there on the first page were two pictures. On the left were two little boys, both holding soccer balls, smiling into the camera.

Underneath that one it read, "Normal vision."

On the right was the other picture, most of the frame black, and all you could see was half of each boy's face, nothing else. That and the black.

Underneath that one it read, "As seen by a person with retinitis pigmentosa."

As seen by Abby.

Abby through the keyhole.

No known cure, the website said, but Nate knew that part already. Knew—even worse—that usually people lived well into their grown-up years before retinitis pigmentosa made them go completely blind. Knew that was the normal progression with the disease. And knew that the form of retinitis pigmentosa that Abby had—Leber's congenital amaurosis—normally attacked kids at birth. Or at least in early childhood.

Only the great Abby McCall couldn't be normal, even when it came to going blind.

So all the doctors and specialists she'd seen had said the same thing, about the onset of Leber's with a thirteen-year-old, how "remarkable" that was. And how "remarkably rapid" the progression of Leber's was with Abby McCall.

Nate just thought it figured, the remarkable part. Just because Abby, now more than ever, was the most remarkable person he'd ever known.

Starting with the fact that even now, even with Nate seeing how much harder things were getting for her, especially in school, Abby acted as if the only thing in the world that mattered was Nate making his throw.

"The key with you," she was saying now, "is getting your brain to work as well as that arm of yours."

"No chance," he said.

This was a couple of days after they'd watched him on SportsCenter, Nate and Abby having walked over to Coppo Park after a teachers' conference half day of school. Coppo Park was one of their favorite places in town, and now they were there. A bench was positioned perfectly in the morning sun, so that even in the middle of winter you could sit without a coat on and re-member what summer felt like.

The sun was so bright this morning, in fact, that Abby was doing something she never did when anybody except Nate was around: wearing the huge wraparound sunglasses with the or-ange tint, ones that reduced the light hitting her eyes and made her feel more comfortable.

Because now the days were becoming as hard for her as the nights. There was hardly any good light for her anymore.

"You're only fired up because you're the one who got me into this," Nate said. "Set me up to choke my brains out in front of the whole stinking country."

"Well, I'll tell you one thing, Mister," she said. "I don't care how bright the stinking stadium lights are that night, I'm not going to be Goggle Girl."

She put her hands on the sides of the sunglasses, like she was a golfer studying a putt.

"I don't know why you hate wearing those glasses so much," he said. "I think you look cool in them."

She shook her head. "I may be blind, Brady," she said. "But I'm not stupid."

Nate hated when Abby said "blind." He thought about it all the time. He just didn't like the word getting out into the air.

"You go ahead and line up all the ways I could describe you," he said. "Stupid would be dead last."

"They make me look like a nerd," she said. "The star of the new series *Ugly Abby*."

"Like that could ever happen."

"You know that's not what I really hate about them," she said.

Just like that, her voice had changed, the way it could when she decided to get serious. "The thing I hate the most is how much they draw attention to me."

"I know."

"I know you know," she said. "It's why you're you and everybody else is everybody else."

One of her favorite expressions.

"Right back at you," Nate said.

Abby grabbed Nate's football off his lap then, got up off the bench and caught her hip on the end of the long picnic table in front of them, which Nate knew had to sting. She was bumping into things more often lately. But she acted as if it hadn't happened.

"C'mon," she said.

"Where are we going?"

"To work on your passing," she said.

"Not one of your more brilliant ideas," he said.

"Ex*cuse* me?" she said. "I thought you said all of my ideas were absolutely brilliant."

She was across the deck now, and whipped a perfect pass at him.

"What's the matter, Brady?" she said. "Afraid people won't be able to tell which one of us throws more like a girl?"

CHAPTER 5

There was no one else on the field. On the other side, way over near the swimming pool, Nate could see people walking their dogs in Coppo's new dog park.

"One condition before we start," Nate said.

"I'm not negotiating, Brady."

"Just one," he said. "You've got to keep the sunglasses on."

Abby said, "They're not going to help me catch the ball."

"If they go," he said, "I go."

"You are not the boss of me."

"True that," Nate said, smiling. "But I am the quarterback, which means I'm the one who gets to call the plays. It's a rule they passed."

"Fine," she said. "But this will cost you down the road."

Nate said, "It always does."

They hadn't played catch together in a long time, and Nate wasn't sure why she was so fixed on doing it today. Maybe it was just because the weather was so beautiful, not summer and not fall, but something right in between. Maybe having a day off from school always felt like you were putting one over on the world. Or maybe, just maybe, this was one of those days when Abby, without coming right out and saying so, just wanted to pretend things were the way they used to be.

The way they were supposed to be.

All Nate knew for sure was this: He was as nervous as if it were third-and-long. Or maybe even fourth-and-goal.

No, that was wrong. Because when he was in situations like that in a game, on a real football field in a real game, when the ball and the game were in his hands, Nate never *really* felt nervous, even though he knew the other guys in the huddle were.

Nate would get excited.

Totally.

But never nervous.

Today he was. He could see how happy Abby was just to be out here with him and he didn't want something—didn't want *anything*—to go wrong.

She moved about twenty yards away from him, clapped her hands, yelled, "Okay, bring it."

"Get closer, Abs."

"No."

"Just a little closer. Please?"

She grinned, took one baby step toward him, and said, "Happy?"

He wanted to tell her that of course he was happy. He was always happy to be with her, on a park field or anywhere else.

But the glasses stopped him.

Nate couldn't help it. She was right about them, they *did* draw attention to her, like some sign she was wearing. Even on what should have been a perfect day like this, those glasses shouted that nothing was going to be normal for her from now on.

"I'm *wait*ing," she said.

Nate took a big step toward her, tossed the ball.

Underhanded.

She caught it with no problem, already shaking her head, saying, "This isn't tosses for tots."

She whipped a perfect spiral right back at him. Not throwing like a girl at all.

Just throwing.

"Put some mustard on the next one, Alice," she said to him, clapping her hands again.

"This is not a contest," he said, but lobbed the next one back to her overhand.

"Better," she said. "But we're not there yet."

Abby McCall was graceful in everything she did before she started to lose her sight, before she couldn't help herself from stumbling or bumping into things or ending up on the ground sometimes. She was her old graceful self now, moving to her right on her long legs, stopping, throwing another beautiful pass back to Nate.

"Oh yeah," she said, doing her own version of a touchdown dance. "Oh yeah. We are playing some ball now."

He threw his next pass a little harder, trying to make it perfect, telling her to focus, watch the ball out of his hands. Making sure it wasn't too low, but wasn't anywhere near her face, either.

Thinking: This is what it's going to feel like on Thanksgiving night.

They threw like this, no problems, for a while, until Nate finally said, "Couple more. I don't want to throw my arm out before the Blair game."

"Right," Abby said. "Wouldn't want that to happen. Because you're putting soooooo much pressure on your throwing arm." She put her hands on her hips. "Who are we kidding here, Brady? You could throw harder with your *left* hand."

"It's not like I don't have to lay it in there all soft for Pete sometimes," he said.

"You know what I love about you?" she said, not embarrassed, not ever embarrassed, to use that word in front of him. "You are as bad at lying as you are good at football."

She laughed then. And even with those glasses on, Nate thought she looked tremendous.

"Okay," she said then. "One more and we're done."

She took off, faking out an imaginary defender, like she was the one running Hutchins-and-Go now, not running at full speed, but running free, long legs eating up the field.

Nate didn't throw this one any harder than the ones before it and was sure he had led her perfectly, as if he were hitting LaDell with a short swing pass coming out of the backfield.

He wasn't sure why she tripped.

Wasn't sure whether there was some little hole in the ground, or one of those uneven places where there was a patch of green that seemed a foot or two higher than anything around it. It's possible that even if she still had two good eyes, she wouldn't have seen whatever tripped her up.

But something did.

Nate saw the whole thing playing out like it was in slow motion, saw her start to stumble, knew she wasn't going to be able to stop herself, saw her pitch forward as she completely lost her balance. And now Nate's throw wasn't leading her the way he'd wanted it to, it was catching her on the side of her head, sending those big sunglasses flying.

Nate ran toward her as soon as she hit the ground, getting to her before the ball had even stopped rolling away.

"Abs, I'm so sorry," he said. "Are you okay?"

"I'm okay," she said in a quiet voice, not sounding scared or hurt or upset. Just quiet.

She looked right at him then, hard as she could, as though she could see everything, everything that had just happened to her, everything that was going to happen.

Then she smiled at him again, bigger than before.

"Thanks, Brady," she said.

"*Thanks?*" he said. "For what?"

She reached up to him with her hand, and Nate helped her up.

"For putting me in the game one more time," she said.

CHAPTER 6

There were times when Nate could actually trick himself into thinking things were the same as they'd always been with his dad. At least, when his dad was around.

They would sit at the kitchen table and talk about last Sunday's Patriots game, unless it was time to start looking ahead to next Sunday's game. They'd talk about Tom Brady's statistics, his touchdowns and interceptions, not that there were ever many interceptions to talk about. They would even discuss Brady's "passer rating," Nate having figured out how to compute a guy's quarterback rating on his own.

Abby said it was the first math homework assignment Nate had ever *wanted* to complete. And she was right.

He had worked on the football math until he got it perfect—the strange formula that used completion percentage, yards per attempt, touchdowns per attempt, and interceptions per attempt. The formula that had a highest possible rating of 158.3.

"Great, Brady," Abby had said the one and only time he tried to explain it to her. "One hundred percent is a perfect score for everybody else, yet you have to go to one fifty-eight just to show off."

"You forgot point three," he'd said.

"Shut up," she'd said.

His dad got it, though. His dad had always had a good head for numbers, even though he joked these days that the numbers weren't adding up for their family quite the way they used to, that it was a good thing nobody was rating him on how he was selling real estate.

Those conversations, the ones about family finances and the state of the real estate business, never lasted very long.

On the rare nights when his dad was home for dinner, they'd head over to Coppo Park as soon as they finished clearing the table and throw a ball around. Chris Brodie had been a quarter-back in high school and still had a decent arm, and when he'd get warmed up, when he'd start to feel loose, Nate would know what it felt like to be Pete or one of his other receivers on the Valley team. What it was like to be on the receiving end, the *pain* end, of what Pete liked to call one of Nate's darts.

On nights like these, Nate's dad would laugh and act as if he didn't have a care in the world.

Only the next night he wouldn't be there for dinner, would be off to his second job as the night manager at Big Bill's Sports in DeWitt, the next town over, in the Pheasant Hill outlet mall just off the highway—a mall that made the one in Valley look small enough to fit in its pocket. The stores there stayed open until ten o'clock. Most nights, Nate's dad wouldn't be home until eleven, by which time Nate would be asleep.

And when Nate would get up for breakfast the next morning, there would be no conversation about sports or anything else at the kitchen table because his dad would already be at the tiny office he kept for Brodie Real Estate over McBride's, the convenience store in Valley where everybody went to buy newspapers and candy. Nate had gone there one time—one time only—and immediately realized that Brodie Real Estate was only his dad, and that his "office" was a desk and a telephone and a small window looking out on Elm Street.

When he'd asked his mom about it later, she'd said, "Your dad still needs a place to go in the morning."

"What does he do there all day by himself?" Nate had asked.

"Sometimes he just waits for the phone to ring," she'd said.

His dad put it another way: said he was just waiting for the game to change, the way he had been waiting for it to change since he'd lost his job at his old real estate company.

"We're like the Patriots," he'd said to Nate. "They were down when Belichick started coaching them, but look where they are now. They're the team to beat pretty much every year now. It'll be our turn again soon."

Nate wondered when "soon" would arrive. He hoped it was before somebody finally bit on the "For Sale" sign that had been in front of their house since the end of last school year.

There was something about that sign that was like Abby's

sunglasses, a reminder that hardly anything in Nate's life—
outside of football—was the way he wanted it to be, or the way
he'd always thought it would be before his dad lost his job and
Abby started to lose her eyesight.

The day the "For Sale" sign first went up, his parents had told
him there was nothing for him to worry about. They were always telling him there was nothing to worry about, that they
wouldn't be leaving Valley, that he wasn't going to have to change
schools, that Valley was too small for him to have to worry about
being far from Abby or any of his other friends. They were just
looking for a smaller house, one that fit what his mom liked to
call their "new circumstances."

Nate had tried to get used to those circumstances, had tried
to get used to always keeping his room clean just in case somebody who might want to buy their house was coming by to look
at it.

That was back when people were still coming by to look
at it.

Some nights he would sit at his bedroom window, not looking
at the stars the way Abby loved to, but looking out at that "For
Sale" sign as though it were his address now—not 127 Spencer
Street, just For Sale, Massachusetts.

He was doing that tonight, a few hours after he'd knocked off
Abby's glasses, unable to sleep. He thought about getting on his
computer and seeing if Abby was still awake, instant-messaging
her the way he did at night when he couldn't sleep or couldn't
figure things out, when his mind seemed to be going in ten dif-

ferent directions at once. She'd figure things out for him or give him a pep talk in those huge letters they used now when they were IM'ing each other, or just make him feel better by using one of her favorite phrases:

Get over it, Brady.

And, just like that, he would.

Abby hadn't been awake tonight and Nate had finally managed to fall asleep when voices from downstairs woke him up.

Nate couldn't tell at first whether his parents were having an argument. He just knew that his dad's voice was loud and he was saying something about how *some*body had better buy their house before the bank got it.

Then he heard his mom tell his dad to lower his voice or he was going to wake Nate.

"Maybe he needs to hear this," he said.

"No, Chris," his mom said, "he doesn't. He's got enough to worry about."

And his dad said, "Do you think he doesn't understand what's going on around here? Do you think the boy doesn't see what's happening to us? Do you think he actually believes us when we tell him not to worry about money? He's too smart for that."

Nate's chest tightened and his hands gripped the blanket

hard. His dad wasn't joking about "For Sale" signs now or any-thing else, not talking about game-changers, not talking about how the Patriots got things turned around. Not pretending that things were going to be the way they used to be.

His mom was doing her best to keep her voice low, as though it could somehow quiet his father's loud one. But Nate heard every word in the still darkness.

"Sports is a job for you now, Chris. Not him. He's just a boy."

His father said nothing at first, and Nate thought it was over, that he could try to somehow get back to sleep.

Only it wasn't over.

Nate heard him loud and clear:

"You know what we could use around here? A million dollars."

CHAPTER 7

Nate loved practice.

Not everybody on his team did. Hardly *anybody* on the team loved practice, because more than anything, football practice was repetition, doing things over and over until you had them right, until you could make the decisions you had to make in the game—not just the quarterback, but everybody—in the tiny amount of time you had to make them.

Coach liked to say, "The biggest myth in the world is the one about *dumb* football players. That comes from people who've never played this game. Because once that ball is snapped, guys all over the field have about two seconds, tops, to decide where they're going and what they have to do. So you'd better be prepared in this game, 'cause it comes at you *fast*. Dumb football players? No such thing."

Nate wanted to be the most prepared guy out there. He figured that made him the opposite of Allen Iverson, who was in one of Nate's all-time favorite YouTube clips, the one where he kept saying "practice"—"We're talkin' about *practice*"—over and over as if it were the dirtiest gutter word in the world.

Nate loved putting on his equipment, making sure his pads

were just right, loved joking with the guys when they were stretching to get themselves warmed up. And he knew that the best part of practice, what Coach called their "team work"—two words, not one—where they'd work on plays until they got them perfect, hadn't even started yet.

The great quarterbacks, Nate knew, were the ones who were most prepared. Starting with his man, Brady. Oh, Nate had read up on all that, on Brady and Peyton Manning, how they loved all their time watching game film and even being in the weight room with the big guys on their team, the linemen and the linebackers. He remembered reading somewhere that even before Brady stepped in for Drew Bledsoe the year the Patriots won that first Super Bowl, Coach Belichick used to say that not only did Brady know all the Patriots' plays and all their options, he knew the *other* team's plays and options better than anybody because he'd run those plays against his own defense in practice.

"He was never surprised," Belichick said about the Tom Brady he knew before everybody else did.

Nate wanted to be that kind of quarterback. Nate *wanted* to put in the work. He knew they had more plays—there were seventy-five in all—than any other eighth-grade team around. He knew they had a whole separate offense run from the shotgun formation when no other team in their league did. Nate learned that the way he learned everything else in Coach's offense—studying as if for a final exam.

Valley's backup quarterback was Eric Gaffney, one of the

team's wideouts and almost as much of a favorite receiver for Nate as Pete Mullaney was. As they were getting ready for practice the Thursday before the Blair game, Nate had been talking about a new play from the shotgun they were going to use on Saturday, and why he thought it would work.

"Coach doesn't even know these plays the way you do," Eric said.

Nate grinned. "I just read the playbook," he said. "Coach wrote it."

"You sure it's not the other way around?" Eric said.

Nate said, "C'mon, if I get hurt or something, you know this stuff as well as I do."

"Dude, no one does." They were finishing warm-ups up now with some hamstring stretches. "And dude?" Eric said. "Please don't get hurt."

Coach Rivers had been a quarterback himself in college, at the University of Massachusetts, and every once in a while he would take a couple of snaps and make a couple of deep throws just to show his players—his words—that he wasn't some kind of "chopper." Tonight he said they were going to start out running plays in their red-zone offense, which meant that Nate and the guys would start on the defense's 20-yard line.

Sometimes they did it that way the last practice before a game, Coach telling them they had two minutes to score. Or a minute. Or even thirty seconds. Sometimes he'd do it the way he did in a game, have his assistant coach for the offense, Coach

Hanratty, hold up a chalkboard with three plays on it, only Nate knowing which one was his "hot read"—the play he was actually going to call.

Sometimes he'd even let Nate call the plays himself.

"The one thing most coaches at this level don't realize," Coach had said the first week of practice, "is that you guys *want* to learn. You're like sponges when it comes to learning. So you'd better know from the jump that we're not going to play your father's style of eighth-grade football. If anybody here thinks ball control means running with it, grab a ball and go run some laps."

Their defensive coach was Coach Burnley, Malcolm's dad. Malcolm pulled double-duty as the Patriots' middle linebacker in addition to playing center.

While he huddled up with his guys, Coach Rivers pulled Nate aside and said, "There's gonna be plays up on the chalkboard, like always. But call what you want tonight, as long as you throw every down."

Nate said, "Well, if you insist."

Then Coach walked away from him, telling everybody that the offense had a minute and a half, no time-outs.

Throw every down, Coach had said.

In Nate's mind, it was like telling a bird to fly.

First down he split out Pete and Eric to the right side, a play they called "L Wait." It meant LaDell. He was supposed to hold his place in the backfield for a couple of beats, then swing out to the left sideline and look for the ball once he crossed the line of scrimmage. If the linebacker came up on him, LaDell could try to blow by him, knowing Nate would read the move.

Nate took the snap from Malcolm, dropped back, rolled a little to his right, trying to make it look as if he had Pete and Eric over on that side of the field for a reason, that he planned to end this imaginary ninety-second game—the best kind of fantasy football—on the very first play.

He eyeballed his wideouts just long enough, then looked to his left, saw LaDell over there, saw their right linebacker, Sam Baum, giving him way too much room, five yards at least, LaDell wide open.

A beautiful thing. LaDell being open that way.

It was the pass that was ugly. Hideously ugly. Nate knew as soon as he released the ball, knew it was a bad throw the way he knew when it was all good. *Knew.* He had given the ball too much hang time, led LaDell by too much. And even though Sam Baum had to be as surprised as anybody on the field that Nate would give him this kind of bunny on the first play of practice—or ever—he knew what to do when he saw the ball floating in front of him like a beach ball.

He closed on the ball as if the play had been called for him, as if he were Nate's primary receiver, and there was nothing LaDell could do to stop him. Sam caught the ball in stride and ran the other way with it until Coach, the only one who *could* stop him, did that by blowing his whistle.

As practice wore on, the harder Nate tried, the harder it got for him to hit what he was aiming at.

When they moved the ball back later, in a part of practice called "Stretching the Field"—you could only try for pass plays of fifteen yards or more—he had Pete wide open on a Hutchins-and-Go and overthrew him by ten yards.

When Pete got back to the huddle, he tried to make a joke of it, saying to Nate, "It was already too high when it went over my head for me to make out what airline it was. Thought it might be jetBlue but, like I said, no way of knowing for sure."

Nate didn't miss everybody by that much. And he didn't miss with every ball he threw. But for the first time all season, practice or game, for the first time in a long time, he felt as if he had borrowed somebody else's arm.

In baseball they talked about "command" with pitchers.

Tonight Nate had no command.

Short passes, long passes, didn't matter. The surprise tonight was when he completed one. When Coach finally gave Eric a few snaps before they finished, the way he always did, he pulled Nate aside and said, "Your arm okay?"

"I'm *feeling* fine," Nate said. "I just feel like my brain and my arm didn't know each other tonight."

"Maybe that was your problem tonight," Coach Rivers said. "Maybe you were just thinking too much."

Nate knew Coach was probably right. What he couldn't figure out was this:

Thinking too much about *what*?

CHAPTER 8

All week long, Nate was expecting his dad to go to the Blair game. Chris Brodie had said he'd switch his schedule around, that instead of working on Saturday this week, he'd work one extra night at Big Bill's the following week.

Nate told his dad he didn't have to do that, give up one of the few times during the week when he could still have dinner with Nate and his mom. He knew what a grind it was for his dad to come home at eleven most nights, then get up the next morning and try to sell real estate.

"I'm not doing it because I have to," his dad had said. "I'm doing it because I've got prime tickets to watch the best thirteen-year-old quarterback in the state."

"Dad," Nate said. "It's just one game."

And his dad had said, "Someday when you have a son who's the quarterback and realize just how few of these Saturdays there really are, you'll understand."

It was eight o'clock Saturday morning when the phone rang, and Nate got a sinking feeling in his stomach. It was the manager at Big Bill's, calling to tell Chris Brodie that the man he'd switched with had called in sick and that Nate's dad was going to have to work that day after all.

Nate could hear only bits and pieces of his dad's side of the conversation, because as soon as his dad knew who it was on the other end of the line, he walked out of the kitchen. But one word Nate kept hearing over and over was "please."

His dad pleading with the man.

When he came back into the kitchen, he said, "I have to work," in a voice that sounded as small as if it were coming from upstairs.

"I'm sorry," he said to Nate.

Then he looked at Nate's mom for a long time, what felt like forever to Nate just because the look on his dad's face was so sad, and said, "I hate this." He walked out of the kitchen again and they heard the slow, heavy sound of him walking up the stairs.

When he came back down, he was wearing the red "Big Bill" shirt that he had to wear to the store, one that Nate knew his dad had come to hate, knew because he had once heard him tell Nate's mom he hated it, that it was like a uniform announcing to everybody what was happening to him.

Like Abby's orange sunglasses.

Blair called themselves the Bears.

"Pretty sure it isn't short for Care Bears," LaDell said when they started their stretching.

"Oh, they care all right," Malcolm said. "Mostly about giving smackdown beatdowns."

"You really think they want to do both?" Nate said.

"Remember last year's game against those suckers?" Pete said. "They thought they *had* given us a smackdown beatdown, and then you hit them with those two long passes in the fourth quarter."

"I remember," Nate said.

He remembered because that was the beauty of sports. There were games you watched and games you played that you knew you'd never forget as long as you lived.

He didn't just remember the two touchdown passes, one to Pete and one to Eric. Nate also remembered how Blair's nose tackle, Willie Clifton, had absolutely laid him out about a half second after Nate had released the ball to LaDell on the conversion that won the game for Valley by one point.

It was a clean hit, nothing illegal about it. Nate still felt as if he'd been dropped out of his bedroom window.

Willie helped him to his feet that day, picked him up as easily as if he were picking up the morning paper in the driveway. And Nate had thought that was pretty good sportsmanship on his part until Willie said, "This isn't over," and walked away.

Nate reminded the guys of that now, saying, "I didn't know whether that meant he was going to wait for me at the bus, or just see us next season."

"Look at him," Malcolm said, knowing he was the one who was going to have to deal with him all day. "If that's two hun dred pounds, I don't want to see what two fifty is going to look like when he gets there."

Pete said, "I think I can actually *hear* him getting bigger."

"Yeah," Nate said, grabbing the ball that he'd left in the grass next to him, "but you know what they say: bigger they are, harder they fall. At least if somebody puts a good block on them."

"Blocking him makes him really mad," Malcolm said. "But I'll do it."

"Thank you," Nate said.

"And try to make sure that when he does do that harder-they-fall thing, he doesn't do the falling on you."

Of course it wasn't just Willie. Blair looked like they had a bunch of guys almost as wide, like the whole front seven on defense was squeezing right up against that two-hundred-pound limit. Nate also knew from last year that they had a quarterback of their own who could throw it around a little, Tyler McCloskey. Tyler could run better than he could throw—he really was Blair's best running back—which made him as hard to defend as any quarterback in their league.

"You know who the *real* bear is for da Bears?" LaDell said, pointing at Tyler. "That sucker right there."

Tyler was warming up on the Blair side of the Valley High School field, throwing one spiral after another as tight as money wadded up in your pocket. Looking nearly as big as everybody else on the Blair Bears, as if he'd shot up a foot since they'd played against him in seventh grade.

"He's big enough to be their tight end now," Nate said.

"Wouldn't help," Pete said. "Even you haven't figured out a way to throw it to yourself."

"Yet," Nate said.

Then the two of them went off to start throwing the ball to each other. And this, even more than the stretching, was the real beginning of Nate's football day. The only thing that would have made it more perfect was if his dad had been able to be here. But at least his mom was here and had picked up Abby on the way. Nate could see them now in the stands, noticing right away that Abby didn't have her sunglasses on, as bright as the day was, and knowing why:

Too many people to see she needed special glasses.

She was looking right at Nate now, as if she were reading his mind, not about the glasses, just knowing he was thinking about her even as he got ready for the best part of his day and the best part of his week.

It wasn't just the football, even though football was a huge part of it.

This was the best part of being a *kid*.

Nate had tried to explain it to Abby one time, fumbling to find the right words—this from a guy who prided himself on hardly ever fumbling on the field—and get her to understand what he meant.

Because, man oh man, talking about your feelings was harder than third-and-long.

"When I'm playing a game," he'd said, "or even just getting ready to play a game, it's like I'm feeling something more than happy. I don't even know what the right word is."

"You just had it, Brady," she'd said. "You just feel *right*."

"So you know what I mean?"

Then she'd gotten this look in those eyes, the ones that were never going to be right, and it was like in that moment she wasn't even looking at him, she was looking at someplace on the other side of him, or way in the distance.

"I know," she'd said.

She waved at him now from the stands. Nate gave her a small wave back and then, because minutes always had a way of turning into seconds when there was a game about to be played, Blair was kicking the ball off and Ben Cion was like a blast of air right up the middle of the field, returning it all the way to the Valley 40-yard line, and Nate was running out onto the field with the guys on offense who hadn't been out there with the kick-return team.

Nate knew that back when Joe Montana was winning Super Bowls with the 49ers, when he was the Tom Brady of his time, that his coach, Bill Walsh, would actually script out the first thirty plays of the game for Montana.

Thirty.

Coach Rivers didn't do that with Valley, but he did always e-mail Nate the night before a game with the ten plays he wanted to use the first time they were on offense, telling him he wanted Nate to picture their first drive of the game, the way they both wanted it to go, inside his head.

"I wouldn't do this with just any thirteen-year-old quarterback," Coach told him one time. "But then, you're not just any thirteen-year-old quarterback."

There would still be three plays up on the chalkboard before every snap, and Coach Hanratty would give Nate a signal like he was a third-base coach letting him know which one was the "hot read," but Nate didn't need the chalkboard for those first ten plays because he had them down cold.

Two running plays to start the game today, then eight straight passes, four with Nate taking the ball from under center, four from the shotgun.

In the first huddle of the day, he called "I-Six," which meant LaDell going through their "six" hole off right tackle, and gave them the snap count.

"Let's play some football," he'd added, like he did before the first snap of every game.

LaDell got eight yards and looked like he might get more before Willie Clifton somehow caught him from behind.

A sweep to the left for Ben, who in addition to returning kickoffs was the Patriots' other running back, got eight more.

First and ten. They were already into Bears territory, their 44-yard line. Just two plays into it and Nate felt as if he had the Bears backing up. Now it was time for a quick hit, a simple slant pass to Pete, coming from Nate's left. It was one of Nate's favorite plays, making him feel as if he were releasing the ball as soon as Malcolm put it in his hands. A quick two-step drop before Nate straightened up and put the ball right on Pete as soon as he got an inside shoulder on the guy covering him.

Only this time he put the ball right on big Willie Clifton.

He didn't know whether Willie had just gotten lucky, straightening up unblocked as Nate backed away from center, dropping back into coverage. Or whether he had somehow been able to read Nate's eyes. But Willie was right in the middle of Nate's passing lane to Pete, and the reason Nate didn't see him was because Willie *wasn't supposed to be there.*

Only he was.

The ball ended up in his hands as if Nate had handed it off to him, and it wasn't one of those deals you saw in NFL games, the big lumbering defensive lineman looking down and acting shocked that the ball was in his hands. Like, *what's this?* Willie acted like he was *supposed* to be there, like he was the one who was supposed to end up with the ball, and just like that, the third play of the game was going the other way. The wrong way. And fast. Because as big as Willie was, he sure hadn't gotten any slower from last season to this.

By the time Nate reacted with his feet, Willie was gone, having cut straight to his right sideline, ten yards clear of everybody in a white uniform.

Including Nate.

Nate chased him all the way to the end zone, as hard as he

could. Pete was running along with him. But they both knew Willie could run like a halfback even though he looked to be twice the size of one.

He beat both of them to the end zone, even looking back over his shoulder at the 5-yard line, not because he was worried they were catching him, just because he could. It was 6–0, Bears, and they hadn't had to run a single play on offense yet.

Willie didn't celebrate once he crossed the line because that would have been like crossing another kind of line in football, one that got you a fifteen-yard penalty the way it did at every other level of football up the ladder from eighth grade. And Willie was cool enough to know that a nose tackle turning around a pass like that, turning it into a touchdown, was much cooler than trying to turn the end zone into some dance routine from *High School Musical*.

He just handed the ball to the nearest ref, slapped five with a few of his teammates who'd finally caught up with the play, and jogged toward the Blair side of the field.

Willie slowed slightly as he passed Nate, who was standing there at the 5-yard line with Pete. Got close enough to Nate to say, "Who wants to be a millionaire, yo?"

CHAPTER 9

The teams were tied 7–7 at halftime. It had hardly anything to do with the way Nate was playing and absolutely nothing—zip, zero—with the way he was throwing the ball.

The Patriots were still in the game *despite* him today.

Because it turned out that the throw to Willie Clifton was one of Nate's better throws of the half, just because it was in the neighborhood of one of his intended receivers. They had come into the game thinking they couldn't run the ball against the Blair Bears because of all that size they had up front, but by the time the Patriots took the ball on a 70-yard drive to tie things up, running the ball was *all* they were doing. In their playbook, the even numbers meant you ran right and the odd numbers meant you ran left, and as they finally started moving the ball, Nate just kept looking over at the chalkboard to see which direction LaDell or Ben would be running. They ran the ball and kept running and that was the script for the Valley Patriots now, not a single pass on the drive that ate up the clock and the field.

"You okay with this?" Coach Rivers had asked Nate before what turned out to be the last drive of the half, telling him what they were going to do, going after a smash-mouth team with smash-mouth ball.

"I'm about winning, Coach, you know that," Nate said. "I'd rather have this many completions"—he made a *0* with his thumb and forefinger—"if that's the best way for us to get a *W*."

"You carry us every Saturday," Coach said. "Let's let 'Dell and Ben do that for a few minutes."

LaDell finally ran it into the end zone from the 5-yard line with fifteen seconds left on a draw play, a thing of beauty, Malcolm just burying Willie for once, everybody else blocking their man as if their starting jobs depended on it, LaDell going straight up the middle untouched.

"Okay," Coach said at halftime. "New ball game."

I *hope*, Nate thought.

He threw free and easy warming up with Pete, throwing the ball to him and then backing up until he was thirty yards away, throwing one spiral after another, Pete never having to move. But he'd felt that way before the game, too. He just wasn't able to carry that feeling into the game.

On their second series of the half, Pete ran a sweet Hutchins-and-Go, smoked the cornerback trying to cover him and left him behind. Nate couldn't believe how open Pete was, just because the cornerback, no. 22, had done such a good job locking him down for most of the game. So Nate wasn't about to overthrow his bud this time, made sure that even if Pete had to wait for the ball, he was going to put his hands on it.

Pete was that kind of open.

Nate released the pass.

And hung the ball up there so long that the Bears' free safety had plenty of time to catch up with Pete.

Pete was so focused on the ball that he never saw the safety coming, just watched helplessly as the kid cut in front of him and picked the ball off and fell out of bounds.

Second interception of the game. First time that had ever happened to Nate Brodie in his life. And when Tyler McCloskey connected deep on the very next play, hitting his wide-open receiver in stride, the Bears were back in the lead.

On the sideline Nate said to Pete, "That interception was even uglier than the first one."

Pete said, "Can I be you for a second?"

"Yeah," Nate said, "but I don't know why anybody would want to be me today."

"What interception?" Pete said. "You understand what I'm saying to you?"

Nate did: forget the bad plays as though he had sports amnesia. The way Coach talked about. The way the pros did.

But forgetting didn't help his aim any. He went out for the next series and threw incompletion after incompletion. He knew he was overthinking his throws, but knowing didn't make it stop.

Fortunately, the Patriots defense was eager to make up for the touchdown they'd allowed on the last drive. Malcolm forced a

Tyler McCloskey fumble on the first play and not only recovered the ball, he returned it all the way for a touchdown.

Just like that, the Patriots were within a point.

In eighth-grade football you got two points for kicking a conversion after a touchdown, but hardly anybody kicked, not even the Patriots. Even as well as Malcolm could snap a ball, Coach knew too many things could go wrong. If you ran it in or passed it in, you got a point. Valley tried to run after Malcolm's score. But even though there looked to be a hole for Ben behind Malcolm and Sam, Willie stepped into it and hit Ben so hard that his helmet ended up sideways.

14–13.

The defenses stiffened and it stayed that way until there were two minutes left. Valley had the ball on their 28 yard line after a Blair punt. Before the offense ran out on the field, Coach said to them, "Short and sweet, boys. The measure of a champ is how he finds his best in the late rounds of the fight. So go find your best now."

Nate knew he wasn't talking to the rest of them as much as he was talking to him. He looked up into the stands for Abby as he ran onto the field, but she wasn't where she had been sitting at the start of the game, and neither was his mom. It wasn't all that unusual, though. He knew both of them liked to walk around sometimes during the game, find a spot they thought would bring Nate some luck.

He sure needed some of that luck now.

Brady time, he told himself.

Let's play football.

The Patriots came out running. It wasn't the drive Nate had always imagined himself leading, but it was effective—and it was his ability to pass that set up the longest run of the day for either team, a twenty-yard scramble on a third-and-twelve from the Blair 29.

Forty seconds left.

One time-out remaining for the Patriots.

They went on a quick-count, hoping to catch the Bears on their heels, and Nate handed off to LaDell, but Willie wasn't fooled. He read the play perfectly and caught LaDell behind the line of scrimmage for a two-yard loss. The Patriots were forced to call their last time-out.

After a quick stop at the sidelines to talk with Coach Rivers, Nate completed a short swing pass to Ben by the right sideline. Ben turned upfield and ran seventeen yards before stepping out of bounds and stopping the clock.

First-and-ten from the Bears' 14-yard line. Fourteen seconds on the clock and no time-outs left. Time for two throws into the end zone. But, Nate knew, get sacked and the game would be over. Nate reminded himself: If I don't see an open receiver, throw the ball away. He almost smiled. It was the one thing he knew he could do with ease today: throw an incompletion over everyone's head.

Nate checked the chalkboard.

The first play was the same slant they'd run for Pete on the third play of the game, the one Willie had picked off. Nobody in the huddle said a word about it. Even now, Nate knew they trusted him.

"On two," Nate said.

Nate took the snap, took his quick drop, froze Willie this time by looking right, like he was throwing to Eric. Then his eyes found Pete, slashing from the left the way he slashed to the basket in hoops, and Nate led him perfectly.

Only, the throw was high.

Pete reached for it, went as high as he could for it, but the ball tipped off his fingers.

Incomplete.

They were down to their last play.

Nine seconds left.

All Nate said to Pete in the huddle was, "I'll apologize later."

He could see Pete grinning on the inside of his face mask. "Will you take me for ice cream, too?"

"Let's beat da Bears first."

He called for a play they called "X-Men." A crossing pattern for Pete and Eric from opposite sides, X being where they passed each other in the middle of the field and—ideally—at least one of them lost the guy covering him.

Nate told the guys in the line he'd take them for ice cream, too, as long as they held their blocks even longer than they had been all day.

"Doable," Malcolm Burnley said.

"'Dell," Nate said, "you know the drill. Sneak out to the right corner of the end zone while I'm eyeballing the other guys."

They went with a quick count, Nate short-stepping back into the pocket, watching his two wideouts close in on each other. But the two Blair cornerbacks read the play perfectly, switching off on their receivers and smothering "X-Men" like they'd thrown a blanket over the sucker.

The line was doing its best to hold their blocks, but Willie had beaten Malcolm and was now coming wide open up the middle at Nate as if a crossing guard had waved him through. Nate couldn't roll to his right, too much traffic over there, so he rolled left, even though his last option—'Dell—was on the other side of the field.

Willie still coming.

Nate rolled, keeping his eyes on the end zone as he did, used those eyes of his and saw LaDell waving his arms from the corner, nobody near him, like he'd found an open spot in the parking lot.

Yeah, Nate thought.

Yeah.

No hesitation now, no doubts, he planted his back foot and threw across his body, let it rip the way he had plenty of times before, when it was just him and the ball and the target.

And threw it over the moon.

The ball ended up about ten feet over LaDell's head. If it were a hit baseball, the ball still rising as it went over the fence, the announcers would have called it a tape measure shot.

Blair 14, Valley 13.

Game over.

Nate stayed where he was, watching the Blair players celebrate around Willie Clifton. Saw everything, just like always, saw the whole field. Saw LaDell, like he didn't know what to do or where to go, jog after the ball Nate had thrown over his head like that was his last job today, the final part of the play.

Finally Nate took as long a walk as he could to the sideline, to where his coach and his teammates were. From the time he'd started playing football, on the days when he got treated like the Next Big Thing in Valley, Mass., and on days when his team fell short, Nate really did believe you won as a team and lost as a team.

Just not today.

Right before he got to Coach Rivers, he took one last look up into the stands, which were already emptying out, one last look for Abby and his mom.

"They're not here," Coach Rivers said. "I decided to wait until the game was over to tell you. Abby fell. Your mom had to take her to the hospital."

CHAPTER 10

Nate didn't have to go to the hospital, which was a good thing. No, a *great* thing, because he hated hospitals even more than he hated losing football games.

Even a game like today, one he somehow managed to lose all by himself.

Coach Rivers used his cell phone to call Nate's mom, and when she answered, he put Nate on the phone right away. His mom told him she and Abby would be leaving the emergency room at St. Joseph's Hospital in a few minutes.

"Caught a break, pal," his mom said. "There was nobody ahead of us, which meant no waiting time. Which, come to think of it, isn't just a break, it's like some kind of miracle, especially on a Saturday . . ."

There were no short answers from his mom, even when Nate hadn't asked a question yet. Nate loved his mom to the sky and back, but she could talk the way Tiger Woods could golf.

"*Mom!*" Nate said, knowing he was interrupting her, snapping at her really, and not caring. He wanted to hear about Abby. "So she wasn't hurt that bad?"

"It was a good bonk on the head, all right. But no stitches because we did a good job with the Band-Aids, just a butterfly bandage to keep the cut closed. For the next week she is going to look like she went a few rounds with Muhammad Ali's daughter, I can never remember her name, the woman boxer . . ."

Nate sighed. "Laila," he said.

"Thanks," his mom said. "Anyway, I'm going to have Coach drop you at Abby's house, and we'll all meet there."

"Just tell me real fast what happened," Nate said.

"She wanted to get closer to the field," his mom said. "Told me her mojo wasn't working from the stands today. If she could get closer to the field, she knew she could get you to stop throwing the ball around—now, these are her words, hon—like a paper airplane."

Even now, with Abby at the hospital, she could still make him feel a little better about everything. "Very nice," he said.

"So she went too fast down the bleachers and wasn't paying attention."

"Down she went."

"Pretty hard."

"Sounds like it could have been worse," Nate said, and his mom said, "Gotta run, the doctor wants to talk to me, see you at Abby's."

She hadn't asked how the game had turned out and Nate hadn't cared, because all of a sudden throwing one over LaDell's head didn't feel nearly as much like the end of the world.

Even if Nate did feel that his favorite day of the week couldn't be going any worse.

Abby's face, always the prettiest one in their class, wasn't pretty today. But Nate did what Abby always did when he became too serious. He made a joke out of it.

"I'm sorry," he said when she opened her front door. "I was looking for Abby McCall."

"Don't try to be funny, Brady," she said. "I'm the funny one."

He grinned, knowing that if he acted for one minute as worried and scared as he had been when Coach told him she'd fallen, she'd make him go sit in his mom's car until it was time for him to go home.

"Yeah, you got me," he said. "You are *definitely* the funny one today."

The cut was over her right eye, the angry-looking bruise on her right cheek. But she was still Abby. "You think so, huh?" she said. "I *did* see most of the game before I did my half gainer."

"Ouch," Nate said.

"My sentiments exactly," Abby said.

She took him back to the kitchen, where their moms were having coffee. Beth McCall had been friends with Nate's mom even before Nate and Abby started hanging around together, were in the same book club now, and used to have a regular doubles match in tennis before the Brodies had to give up their membership at Valley Country Club.

Sue Brodie looked over to them now and said, "The dynamic duo rides again."

"Kind of a bumpy ride today," Abby said.

"For both of us," Nate said.

Nate's mom said, "The mothers should be as resilient as the children."

"Half," Abby's mom said.

"Everybody doing okay for the time being?" Nate's mom asked.

"Sort of," Nate said. "I was just thinking that I kind of did to my team what happened to Abs. Threw 'em right down a flight of stairs."

"Everybody has a bad day once in a while," Mrs. McCall said. "Even the best eighth-grade quarterback in the state."

"The only state I was in today was the state of I-stink," Nate said.

"The state of I-stink." Abby laughed. "Now *that* was funny."

"You see what it's like for me?" Nate said. "It's good that I didn't come here looking for any sympathy."

"Never," Abby said. "You know my deal: If you're looking for sympathy, buy yourself a Hallmark card. Now let's bounce."

She led him up the back stairs to her room. Two rooms, actually. There was her bedroom, and then attached to the bedroom was what had been her playroom when she was little, but now had become her art studio, where she came to draw and paint. It was the one place—or at least Nate thought so—where the world she saw was still bright and full of colors. Colors he had never seen anywhere else.

No two paintings were the same. There was one of a forest, but not like any Nate had ever seen. It looked to him like the most brightly colored rain forest in the world. There was one of a big city, Nate guessing it was Boston, but the way a city would look if you saw it through a kaleidoscope.

There was one that showed a beach and an ocean beyond it, the water a shade of blue like none Nate had ever seen, making him think that Abby was like some mad scientist with colors, mixing them to come up with something brand new.

Scattered all over the floor were open sketchbooks, most showing pencil sketches, all of faces. There was Malcolm captured perfectly, Pete, even Mr. Doherty, their English teacher at school.

In the corner, set up on an easel, there was one of Nate.

When Abby saw him looking in that direction, she made a quick move over there, nearly knocking down an easel on the way as though it wasn't there.

"Not done yet," she said.

"You make it sound like something you're baking," Nate said.

She smiled right through her bumps and bruises and the bandage on her head. "Half-baked," she said, "just like you."

"I would have settled for half-baked today," he said. "Because if I'd played even *half* as good as I usually do, we would've won."

Abby could tell the time for joking about the game was over. In a quiet voice she said, "I'm sorry you lost."

"Not as sorry as I am that you fell."

"So we both fell today, Brady. But who's better at bouncing right back up than us?"

He sat down in one of those canvas chairs that was supposed to look like the kind Hollywood directors sat in on movie sets, one with "Nate" written on the back. Abby had given it to him on his last birthday, but then told him he wasn't allowed to keep it at home; it was going in her studio.

"I still can't believe I have my very own reserved seat," he said.

"It's like I explained to you," she said. "Since you're the only one allowed in here on a regular basis, you might as well have your own viewing chair."

"It's a great view," he said.

"While it lasts," Abby answered, a little too quickly.

"You're gonna be fine, Abs," Nate said.

"That's my line," she said. And she smiled again, only this one was different. "Or maybe I should say that's my *lie*."

The room was quiet now, except for some music coming from her bedroom. Abby was on the floor, legs crossed, jeans still dirty from where she must have hit the ground, her hand moving all over the page on the sketch pad she'd grabbed, a blur like it always was. Not looking up at him, concentrating.

Nate asked, "What really happened today?"

"It's like I heard your mom telling you," she said. "You know how sometimes I'm at one of your games and I mind-meld you and get you to look over?"

"Yeah," he said.

"Well, it wasn't working well enough today from where I was sitting." She gave a quick look up. "You know this isn't crazy, right?"

"Never," he said.

"So I thought I needed to get closer to you today, so I could just give you a look that said, *Chill, dopeface*." Abby went back to her drawing now, shaking her head as she did. "I've never seen you that uptight over anything except maybe a Spanish test."

"Tell me about it."

"So here's what I'm wondering," she said. *"Why?"*

"I thought we were talking about the bleachers reaching out and tripping you."

Nate didn't want to answer the question about the Blair game because he didn't *have* an answer. He didn't know why he'd been pressing so much lately.

"Yes, we were talking about that." She sighed and said, "It was just another time, like when we were playing catch the other day, that I was dumb enough to think I can do things like I used to. So now I'm dumb and blind. Thinking I could take the bleachers two at a time, because I was in such a rush to get down to you. I missed the second-to-last one and fell sideways, like I was the lead of the dork parade."

The pad was still in her lap, one of her special drawing pencils from the art store in her right hand. Her hand was still for a change. The music had stopped in her bedroom.

"I'm glad you tried," he said. "I needed you."

"I know," she said.

They were silent for a minute.

Then Abby said, "You know how you couldn't play the way you wanted to today, no matter how hard you tried?"

"Oh yeah."

"Well, sometimes I can't do this."

"Draw, you mean?"

She looked up at him, looked at him with big eyes that would look perfect to anybody who didn't know what was happening behind them, eyes that were as blue to Nate as the blue water in her painting.

"No, I can still draw."

"Then I don't understand, Abs."

Not the first time he'd said *that* to her.

"I mean, sometimes I'm no good at going blind."

CHAPTER 11

Nate's favorite place to throw a football, at least when he wanted to go off and do it alone, was at a corner of Coppo Field that most kids had forgotten, on the far side of the new dog park.

That's where the tire was.

It hung from this low, thick branch on what Nate thought had to be the oldest oak tree on the whole property and had been there from the time Nate first started coming to the park. This was where the playground had been at Coppo before they had given the place a big expensive makeover, putting in the dog park, building a newer and better and more expensive playground over on the other side of the soccer fields. Nate's mom used to take him there when he was little, both of them knowing he would get tired of the swings and slides and monkey bars pretty quickly. That's why he always brought a football with him, whatever one he could grip at the time, and entertained himself throwing the ball—or trying to, anyway—through the big old tire that looked as old as the tree.

After dinner that night, his dad still not home because he was working an extra shift, Nate rode his bike over to Coppo to throw.

Just because he didn't want to go to bed that night and have his last football thing of the day, of the week, be the ball he'd sailed over LaDell's head when a good throw would've beat the Blair Bears.

He could still hear Willie Clifton burning on him after his *first* bad throw of the day, Willie saying, "Who wants to be a million-aire, yo?"

Like the Million-Dollar Throw had anything to do with what had happened on the field today.

"Even Brady has had bad games, Brady," is the way Abby put it before he left her studio.

His mom had told him the same thing over dinner, in about ten different ways.

"If your father were here," she'd finally said, "he could take care of this with a single sentence."

But he wasn't there and he hadn't been at the game and he'd called when they got home from Abby's to tell them not to hold dinner. Which was actually fine with Nate. He didn't want any more words of wisdom or consolation tonight, didn't want another person trying to draw a smiley face on a sludge day.

He just wanted to throw.

For just a few minutes before dark, Nate wanted to go someplace—*be* someplace—where the only problem in his life was trying to put a ball through the hole in a tire that was so old now that you could only see the two O's from "Goodyear" written on it. He didn't want to worry about the Million-Dollar Throw or money or his dad's job or the way he'd stunk it up today.

Didn't even want to worry about Abby, just for a little while.

He just wanted to grip it and rip it.

He brought one of his favorite balls with him, an old regulation NFL ball that had the name of the previous commissioner, Paul Tagliabue, on it. The ball had some miles on it, and Nate didn't think the laces were going to last much longer, but it still fit his hand like a batting glove.

There were a bunch of other balls in the old milk crate in the garage, but when Nate was really serious about throwing, he brought only one ball with him. If you brought only one, every throw meant something as you tried to put it through the tire and hit the trunk of the tree squarely, which meant no chasing after it in the woods. Miss the tire, miss the tree. When his dad was still playing golf at Valley Country Club, Nate would watch him on the putting green sometimes, and his dad would be using only one ball while everybody else was using two or three.

Nate asked him why one time and his dad had said, "Because you only get to use one when the putt matters."

Nate warmed up, throwing easy ten-yard passes, putting just about every one through the hole. Then, slowly, he began to move back until he was thirty yards away, knowing that was the distance for the Million-Dollar Throw, knowing he had been fooling himself on the way over, that with everything he told himself he wanted to get out of his head tonight, that throw was never out of his head these days. Not for very long, at least.

Same distance at Coppo he'd have at Gillette Stadium, just with a much bigger target.

Nate took a deep breath now, imagining this was the big night. The biggest throw of his life. Of *any* thirteen-year-old's life, with the whole world watching and a fortune on the line.

Nate imagined Gillette Stadium being as quiet as Coppo Field was right now in the twilight.

He took another deep breath, closed his eyes, remembering as he did so another thing his dad had told him once when he was still golfing, about Jack Nicklaus, whom Nate knew was Tiger Woods before Tiger Woods. His dad said that Nicklaus never stroked a putt until he had already pictured himself making it.

Nate relaxed his shoulders, gave them a little shake like he did over center sometimes, the ball in his right hand, then took one step forward, striding into the throw, and put the ball through the tire.

Nothing but air.

"Arm looks fine to me."

His dad.

He had changed out of his Big Bill shirt and khaki pants, put on the kind of hooded gray sweatshirt that Coach Belichick wore during Patriots games. He was wearing old jeans with paint on them and his old gray New Balance running shoes, which he sometimes said he should be using to run from one job to the next.

Nate said, "*Now* it looks fine."

He jogged over to retrieve the ball at the base of the tree and came back to where his dad was standing.

"Dad," Nate said, "I couldn't do anything right today. I'm *glad* you couldn't come."

"I'm not," his dad said in a quiet voice.

"I'm just saying," Nate said.

"Heard the whole story from your mom." His dad managed a smile. "In great detail."

"Sorry," Nate said.

His dad said, "You ever think Mom is harboring some secret dream to be a play-by-play announcer?"

"But not just in football," Nate said. "I think she'd be happy doing play-by-play for, like, the whole *planet*."

"She told me about the game," his dad said. "And about Abby."

"Not a great day."

"Happens."

"Not like it happened to me in the game today," Nate said. "Dad, I've lost games before, but I've never felt as much like I'd let everybody down."

"You'll get up, though. You always do."

"What are you doing here, by the way?"

"Your mom informed me that you needed company even though she said you didn't *think* you needed company."

"Maybe she was right."

"Oh no, big boy. Not maybe. Our story is going to be that she was definitely right, that you were thrilled to see your old man, and that she still knows you better than anybody. It'll make her whole week."

He put out his fist and Nate gave him some back. "I'm totally down with that," he said.

"Trouble is, you still *look* down."

Maybe it was everything that had happened, because of the game and Abby. Or maybe it was just because it was him and his dad on a field alone and it never seemed to happen that way anymore, at least not as much as Nate *wanted* it to happen.

But it just came out of him, like a genie jumping out of a bottle.

"Why'd they have to pick me to make this stupid throw?"

His dad didn't act surprised, or startled, just made a casual motion for Nate to toss him the ball. Nate did. And then, barely looking at the target, his dad whipped a throw at the tire from the Million-Dollar Throw distance, nearly putting it through on the first try, hitting the side of the tire so hard it spun the thing around.

"Is *that* what all this moping is about?" his dad asked.

"I didn't think I was moping."

"Looks like it to me."

Nate didn't know what to say to that, so he ran after the ball and brought it back. "I mean, I'm excited about doing it, at least some of the time, when I'm not geeked out of my head about it," Nate said. "But most of the time, it's like it's one more thing I don't need right now. Like one more guy piling on when I'm already down."

In a voice that wasn't much louder than the wind at the tops of the trees, his dad said, "When you're down."

"Yeah," Nate said.

"So the thing that's bringing you down," his dad said, "is the chance to do something you'd rather do than eat: throw a football. Live out every kid's dream and maybe win a million dollars doing it. You're telling me *that's* what has your insides tied up in a sailor's knot?"

"No," Nate said, not liking his dad's tone now, not liking the way this was going, wondering how things could get sideways between them this quickly. *"No,"* Nate said. "I didn't mean it like that. I just meant that it's like more pressure than I need right now, that's all."

"Pressure?" his dad said.

And in that moment, it sounded like Iverson talking about "practice." As if Nate had not just said a bad word, he'd let one slip out in front of a parent.

"You're under too much pressure?" his dad said.

His voice sounding completely different from when he'd first shown up at Coppo.

Like it belonged to somebody else.

Nate just stood there, not knowing how to talk to this dad.

"You know what pressure is?" Chris Brodie said. "Pressure is not even getting the chance to do anything you love anymore. Or even like."

"Dad, I get that, I really do."

Nate felt like he was standing there against a blitz he hadn't seen coming.

"Do you get it?" his dad said. "Because I'm not sure you do. I'm not sure anybody does. *Pressure?*" he said again. "Pressure is doing a job you hate, that even makes you hate sports sometimes, so you can hold on to what's supposed to be your real job, except you can't make a living at that job anymore."

Nate looked down and saw him clenching his fists now, unclenching them, over and over, those big hands of his, ones Nate always thought could grip a football as easily as if it were a baseball.

"Dad, I didn't mean to make you mad," Nate said. "I don't even know how we got to talking about this." Just wanting the conversation to be over, just wanting to go home so that what was now officially an all-time, historically bad, *epically* bad Saturday could finally be over. "I know you've had a bad day, way worse than mine . . ."

His dad, shaking his head, like he was locked in now, said, "Pressure is never having enough money and starting to think you're never going to have enough again."

Then, as quickly as he had started, he was finished. He said he'd see Nate at home and started walking across the soccer fields toward the parking lot, Nate watching him until it was as if he had just walked off into the night.

Nate stood there, not moving, feeling the same way he had after the ball had gone over LaDell's head. No. Feeling even worse now.

And Nate knew the real reason he was feeling this lousy was how sorry he was feeling for himself. Because of the way he'd complained about pressure. Whined about it, really. Because of the way his dad had called him out on it.

He wondered what Abby would think of him right now. Abby who never complained, even facing the worst kind of pressure in the world.

She came close sometimes. How could she not? She had come close today when she had admitted to Nate that she just plain stank at going blind.

But Abby McCall, who *was* going blind, never felt as sorry for herself as Nate did right now at Coppo.

It's not Dad I don't know today, he thought.

It's *me*.

CHAPTER 12

Nate didn't watch the Patriots-Jets game with his dad on Sunday even though his dad had the day off. Mostly because he was having as hard a time letting go of the things that had been said the night before as he was the Blair game.

This was a time, he decided, when that sports amnesia Coach liked to talk about wasn't working at all, when he couldn't forget what he wanted to forget, and wasn't even sure he really did want to.

So instead of watching football the way he usually did on Sundays, he went over to Abby's. Abby had a new toy she wanted in the worst way to show off that made it easier for her to read.

"You have *got* to see this thing," she said over the telephone, Nate glad that at least somebody sounded happy about something this weekend. "It is fresh to *death*."

It was called a knfb Mobile Reader, and as soon as Nate saw it, he thought it had to be some kind of trick, because it didn't look like a "mobile reader" at all. It just looked like your regulation cell phone.

It wasn't a trick. And turned out to be a lot more than that to Abby, for whom reading and books had become more and more of a problem, especially when it came to homework assignments. Now here she was with a gadget that was like some kind of magic wand she could wave over books and have them talk to her.

They went up to her room and she showed Nate how she could activate the Mobile Reader with the push of a single button. Then put the phone, which was really like a scanner, over the page of the book they were reading right now in English for Mr. Doherty, *The Diary of Anne Frank*.

She handed the Mobile Reader to Nate.

"Check it out, Brady," she said, as proud as if she'd invented the thing herself, pressing another button. "It's the ultimate in text messaging. From Anne Frank to me."

Nate put the magic gadget to his ear and heard the same page Abby had just scanned being read to him, only it wasn't the voice of the girl Nate had imagined when he was reading, when he'd heard the story inside his head. It was a man.

"This sounds like the voice of Batman on the cartoon show," Nate said.

"Missing the point, Brady," she said. "Not an altogether uncommon experience for you."

"He's *talking* about Anne hiding with her family," Nate said. "But he *sounds* like he should be telling Alfred the butler to fire up the Batmobile. Even though the Batmobile that Bale drives in the movie is a lot cooler than the one in the TV show, frankly."

"And here I was afraid this thing was going to be wasted on you," she said. "You're just not a gadget guy."

"I still can't believe they can use a headset in football to send in plays to the quarterback," he said.

"This is my way of getting books sent in to *me*," she said. "Mr. Doherty says that I can use this in class when we do classroom reading and he wants us to write an instant synopsis when we're done."

"It's like your own audiobook," Nate said.

"I could have gotten *Anne Frank* as an audiobook," Abby said. "But not all the books on our reading list are available as audiobooks. This way, they're *all* available."

"It's cool, Abs, it really is. The coolest. Like you."

He made sure to sound excited because she was excited, like she'd gotten a surprise, a didn't-even-ask-for-it present on Christmas. And Nate knew that the Mobile Reader now meant she wasn't going to need the magnifying computer screen on her desk in English, something Mr. Doherty had discussed with Abby's parents, something that would have been yet one more cause of embarrassment for her.

"I know I'm turning into a special-needs kid," she'd said to Nate. "I just hate when I have to advertise it."

"You know what's going to happen, right?" Nate said. "All the other kids in class are going to want their own Mobile Readers. Total status deal. It's going to be like you showed up with some kind of new iPhone that isn't even in the stores yet."

Abby, her face serious now, said, "I *need* it, Brady. I was starting to fall seriously behind. That's me, though, isn't it? Getting good at falling. Down at football games, behind in school."

"Abs, you're the smartest kid in our grade and everybody knows it. If you're falling behind a little, it just means you're leveling the playing field for everybody else."

"We both hate being behind," she said.

"Yeah," he said.

She cocked her head a little to the side, as if she'd heard something. More and more lately, Nate was starting to believe all the things he'd ever read or heard about people losing their eyesight and having their other senses become new and improved. More *acute*, that was the word people used to describe it. He was seeing it with Abby, with her hearing most of all, like it was superhero acute these days. If there was something even slightly off in Nate's voice, no matter what they happened to be talking about, she jumped all over it.

She could still see right through him, of course, no failing vision there.

"You okay about yesterday's game?"

"Fine."

"What?"

"*What* what? I said I was fine."

"Something's not fine today. Starting with the fact that you're here instead of watching your guy."

"I was footballed out."

"On what planet?"

"Really."

"You think you can fool the all-knowing, all-seeing Oz? Even if Oz needs reading gizmos now?"

"Abs, I'm fine!"

"Are not."

He grabbed the Mobile Reader out of her hand, started talking into it in his own deep Batman voice. "It turns out Nate Brodie did suffer a minor injury during yesterday's Valley-Blair game," he said, "but only to his ego."

"Did something happen after you left here yesterday?"

Nate laughed now. Loudly. Not a sound he expected to be making today, but there it was. "I give," he said, and told her about what had happened the night before.

The things his dad had said.

"Maybe that was just his way of saying 'I give,'" Abby said when he was finished.

"He sounded more beaten than I felt," Nate said. "It's why I was only mad at myself after. I must have sounded to him like the biggest whiner boy in the universe."

"Nope," she said. "Not your style, Brady."

"Abs," he said. "You know what you said yesterday about being no good at . . . what's happening with your eyes?"

She nodded, eyes right on him.

"Well," he said, "sometimes I'm *really* lousy at acting excited about making this throw when there's so much lousy stuff going on around me. And instead of feeling excited, what I really feel is guilty."

Abby grabbed for the Mobile Reader, taking it back from him, and began speaking into it like it was a microphone.

"Earth to Brady," she said. "That is absolutely not allowed."

"I just want you to understand," he said.

She smiled now.

"I do," she said. "But *you* need to understand something, about why you're not allowed to feel guilty, about why you should be marking off the days to this throw like you're marking off days on a Christmas calendar."

"Why is that?"

"Because that throw is the one good thing for all of us right now," she said. "Your dad and me and everybody. That throw isn't just for the money, it's for something a lot more valuable than that."

Nate smiled back at her.

"I give," he said. "Again."

"That throw is the thing that we all gotta believe in, Brady, what keeps us all going," Abby said. "That great things can still happen."

CHAPTER 13

He wasn't going to say this to Abby or his mom or to any of his teammates. He *definitely* wasn't going to say this to his dad, figuring it might get him grounded until he was old enough to have his driver's license.

But whatever pressure Nate was feeling last Saturday didn't amount to a pile of dirty socks compared with what he was feeling *this* Saturday against the Manorville Rams.

It wasn't just that Manorville was loaded this season, a favorite along with Valley to win their league. It wasn't just that Nate, more than ever, wanted to do well in front of his dad, who had been given the day off from Big Bill's and would be coming to the game.

There were a few other people in the crowd Nate wanted to impress, in the worst way:

People from *The Today Show* were there to do a feature on him, and a reporter from *Sports Illustrated* was on hand to write a piece about the eighth-grade quarterback who was going to throw a ball for all that money on Thanksgiving night.

On the way to the game Abby had said, "I used to tell people

I was your publicist. But it's sort of starting to look as if you don't need one, Brady."

They were in the backseat of the used Taurus Nate's dad had been driving lately, this car a lot smaller than the Cherokee they used to have.

Nate said, "And this would be your way of trying to relax me?"

Abby said, "I think the only people *not* here today are *Entertainment Tonight* and *Access Hollywood.*"

She looked as happy sitting next to him as if they were going to a party or to the mall.

"Can I be serious for a second?" Nate said.

"No," she said. "Are you serious about being serious? This is *way* too much fun."

"The thing that sketches me out about the whole thing," Nate said, "is that usually you have to actually *do* something to get this kind of attention. I'm just a guy who got his name picked out of a hat, basically. It's not like I did anything to deserve this."

"Okay, now I'm gonna be serious, but only for a second," Abby said. "*You* don't get to decide stuff like that. Nobody gets to decide who deserves anything."

She turned and looked out the window when she said the last part. She certainly had a point. The last person who deserved what was happening was Abby.

He decided to change the subject.

"One promise today, Abs? No sudden moves into the open field. Or the open bleachers."

"Good one, Brady. Now *you* make *me* a promise, or I may have to beat on you until we get to the field."

Nate went into a crouch, even with his seat belt fastened, like a fighter trying not to get punched. "No," he said. "Please don't hurt me."

"You know how you're always going on and on about how good I am with color?" she said. "How about you make sure you're throwing to the right color uniforms today?"

"Sounds like a plan," he said.

Abby turned now in the backseat, facing Nate, and patted her heart twice. "No kidding around?" she said. "You're going to be great today."

Nate always trusted Abby on everything, on big things and small things and just about everything in between.

He wanted to trust her today more than he ever had.

It was another home game for Valley, so they were in their white uniforms. Manorville wore the same cool deep blue that the St. Louis Rams did, even had ram horns on the sides of their helmets. Last year Valley had beaten them in the last game of the regular season to knock them out of a shot at the league championship, number one versus number two, same as this year. Nate had thrown three touchdown passes that day and run for another and even scored two of their conversions himself. He had as much of what he called a "No. 12 day"—a Brady day—as he'd ever had in his life.

The difference between that day and today, he was thinking halfway through the second quarter, was that the last time he'd faced the Manorville Rams, he hadn't felt as if the whole world were watching every move he made, whether he was on the field or on the sidelines or just getting a drink of Gatorade.

It made him think of one of Malcolm's favorite expressions, from when they'd be hating on a video or a homework assignment or sometimes a player on the other team who was annoying them: He felt like he ought to be sipping on some "Hater-ade," because he was righteously hating all the attention, the idea that he was being followed and that there was nowhere for him to hide. And knowing at the same time that his mood wasn't lousy just because of the TV crew and the reporter from *SI*, but because he was just one-for-eight so far in the game and that one was a four-yard completion to his tight end, Bradley Jacob, that he could have thrown lefty.

All week long he had tried to make a joke out of the Blair game, at least when he was with his teammates, and they had done the same with him as a way of putting it behind all of them. Pete even called the game *The Blair Glitch Project*, after the old movie, telling Nate that his version was scarier than the original.

Now the first quarter and a half of the Manorville game was beginning to feel like a sequel.

Valley was winning, but only because of their defense. Malcolm and Sam seemed to be all over the field on just about every play, disrupting everything Manorville tried to do on offense. It was Sam who caused the fumble that set up a twenty-yard touchdown run by LaDell. And Malcolm who batted away a fourth-down pass from the Valley 2-yard line, keeping the game at 7–0 for Valley.

So Manorville, who had as many weapons on offense as Valley did, including the best running back their age in the state—a kid as big as a nose tackle, named Johnny Farr—was having as much trouble putting the ball into the end zone as Nate was.

But none of that was making Nate feel any better.

Because the more throws he missed, the more he felt as if he had a giant spotlight on him. No matter how hard he tried, he kept looking over to the sidelines to where the cameraman from *Today* was, seeing him at one end of the bench or the other, watching him run down behind the goalposts one time.

With six minutes left in the half, the Patriots began a drive on their 35-yard line. On first down Nate threw the ball downfield on a fade route, missing badly, the ball not anywhere near Pete, landing ten yards out of bounds. On second down he went with a short pass, a little five-yard curl, and bounced the ball in front of Bradley this time. Looking over to the sideline and seeing the camera right on him, again, Nate wondered if the camera could see right inside him the way Abby could.

With the defense expecting another pass on third-and-ten, Coach Hanratty crossed them up and called for a running play, LaDell finding a big enough opening, right up the middle, for fifteen yards and a first down. Nate saw the rest of the guys on offense breaking into smiles as they huddled up. Nate wasn't smiling, though. He wanted to disappear.

And he pretty much *did* disappear after LaDell's run, because Coach Hanratty stayed on the ground now, calling running play after running play. Nate might have had no confidence at that moment, but Malcolm and the boys up front had, and they were suddenly opening up holes big enough to drive school buses right through.

Ben ran for twenty more yards.

Then LaDell took a pitch—Nate could still throw under-handed, like he was with Abby in the park—and ran for twelve more.

The Patriots finally ended up at the Manorville 15-yard line, third-and-eight, ninety seconds left in the first half, a chance to go up two touchdowns on a day when Nate had been sailing the ball around the field like it was a Frisbee.

The hot read on the board was the second one:

"FadE."

Capital *E* on the end, for Eric Gaffney. He would split out by himself on the right side, drive hard to the middle of the field on the cornerback covering him, really selling the fake, even trying to get an inside shoulder on the guy. Once he did, once he had a step on him, he was supposed to fade back in the other direction, toward the right corner of the end zone.

That was the play Nate relayed to his teammates in the huddle, telling Malcolm to snap him the ball on the first sound he made and for everybody to be paying attention. Everybody nodded, knowing it was a perfect play to run in this situation.

Everybody ran it to perfection.

Everybody except Nate, that is.

He took two steps back, carrying the ball high toward his right shoulder, dropping back into the pocket. Yet those two steps were as far as he was going in that direction, because Nate Brodie had no intention of passing the ball.

He waited just long enough to sell the fake, even to his own teammates. Then he took off running. He could have sworn he heard Malcolm yell, "What the . . ." as Nate ran right past his block.

Nate saw only open field in front of him. The only Manorville Ram with a decent shot at him was the middle linebacker, who'd backed up into coverage, trying to spot LaDell as he'd circled out of the backfield. When the linebacker realized it wasn't a pass, saw Nate running open throttle at him down the middle of the field as if he planned to right run through the goalposts, he got his feet tangled up and nearly went down.

Nate didn't even need to juke the guy to glide right past him, almost like he was riding a wave.

So Nate went into the end zone untouched, tossed the ball to the nearest ref, and ran right for Eric Gaffney, standing in the corner of the end zone, no blue jersey even close to him.

"Sorry, dude," Nate said.

"*Sorry?*" Eric Gaffney said. "That audible was dirtier than a *sewer*."

"It's not an audible when only one guy knows the play," Nate said.

"Long as the one guy is our QB." Eric grinned. "And long as it works, of course."

Then Malcolm had Nate in a bear hug, carrying him to the sidelines, Nate finally telling his center to put him down or they were going to get an excessive celebration penalty.

"Brilliance," Malcolm said. "Sketchin', kickin' brilliance."

Nate just shrugged, like it was no big deal. There was still a whole half to play. No point in telling Malcolm or Eric or any of his teammates that brilliance had nothing to do with it.

Wasn't even a factor.

Fear factor was more like it.

Their quarterback had just been afraid to put the ball up.

CHAPTER 14

Valley didn't score in the third quarter. But they didn't have to, because the defense continued to be everything on this day that Nate was not: confident, aggressive. Almost arrogant. Coach Burnley always told them that there had to be a level of arrogance in sports, not acting like you were better than the other guy or showing him up, just *believing* that you were, on every single snap of the ball. That's the way Malcolm and Sam and all the up-front guys were playing today, and when they weren't, the guys in the defensive backfield kept coming up and making big stops themselves.

On offense, Nate was content to put the ball in LaDell's belly, hand it off to him or Ben or even Eric when Coach Hanratty would have three backs lined up behind Nate. He wasn't taking any chances with his play calls, protecting a fourteen-point lead that seemed twice that much the longer the game went on.

Nate hadn't forgotten why the television crew was at the game. He saw the *Sports Illustrated* writer hanging around their sideline. Nate felt them watching every move he made even as he tried to ignore them, reminding himself it was only going to be like this for this one Saturday, that he just had to deal with it until the end of the game.

He told himself that Tom Brady's whole life was having cameras and reporters all around him, all eyes on him, even when he went to visit his girlfriend in New York City, even when he was bringing her flowers.

But there were times when he was standing with the coaches, when the Valley defense was on the field giving Manorville another three-and-out series, that Nate had the urge to turn around, look right into the camera and say, "You're following the wrong guy."

But he didn't.

He just kept cheering on his defense, then running back on the field with the offense, killing a little more clock, getting deeper into the game, never letting on to anybody how much it was killing him inside to play football this way, as if the forward pass hadn't been invented yet.

Valley finally faced a third-and-one. Only a couple of weeks ago, Nate would have loved a moment like this, knowing the defense would be afraid to stack the line on him, knowing that if they did, the best thirteen-year-old quarterback around could go to a play fake and put the ball in the air and end the game right there.

But not today.

Everybody knew Valley was going to run the ball again. So the Rams did stack the line, and stuffed LaDell for no gain, and Valley was forced to punt.

And then Manorville's punt returner, the smallest kid in the game, broke off a return that seemed to go for about 150 yards because of the way he kept crisscrossing the field. Even Nate felt a cheer rise up inside him when he crossed the goal line and promptly sat down in the grass, as if he was too exhausted to do anything else.

If that wasn't enough of a shock, Nate watched as Manorville lined up to *kick* the conversion, and watched their kicker drill the ball through the uprights for two points, and just like that it wasn't 14–0 for Valley anymore, it was 14–8.

A one-touchdown game, with three minutes left, and with Manorville believing in themselves again. All of a sudden Nate knew the Patriots couldn't be content to just run the ball three times and kill a couple of minutes of clock before punting. The Rams still had all of their time-outs. If the Patriots didn't want to give them the ball back, give them a chance to win the game, the Patriots had to make first downs.

Even if it meant throwing to do that.

"We're not going to sit back," Coach Rivers said before Nate went back out with the offense. "I probably did that for too long today, just because your old coach fell in love with his defense."

Nate tried to act more confident than he felt. "You know

our deal, Coach," he said. "You call the plays and I'll run the suckers."

"We're going to play like it's tied," Coach said. "That means for the rest of this game, we're going to play to win."

"Like you always say," Nate said. "Hit them with the whole playbook if we have to."

Except Manorville hit them first. LaDell got stuffed for a five-yard loss on first down, the Rams' middle linebacker walking right into their backfield as if somebody had given him a hall pass. So on second down and fifteen, the play called for a quick crossing route to Bradley, with Nate hopefully hitting him in stride. The throw wasn't horrible—but it was behind Bradley, who tried to reach back with his right hand and control the ball, yet couldn't.

The game clock stopped with the incompletion.

Third-and-fifteen.

Nate looked over for the hot read on Coach Hanratty's board.

It said, "Big Ben."

It meant Ben Cion on a great big fly pattern. All the wide receivers would be on the right side and Ben would line up in the right slot, between the receivers and the offensive line. He would wait as Nate dropped back as though he were staying in to block, then run across the line of scrimmage toward the left sideline before turning it on, flying down the sideline, flaps down.

Nate loved the call. *Let's do this,* he thought.

He couldn't do anything about the other throws today.

Yet he could make *this* throw.

He took a deep breath before leaning down into the huddle with the play, looked past his own bench, past the TV crew and the *Sports Illustrated* writer standing right next to them, up into the stands where Abby was sitting between Nate's mom and dad.

Nate wasn't sure anymore what she could see from long distances, what she could see *period,* but she seemed to see him just fine right now the way he could see her.

Smiling and patting her heart.

Nate did the same.

He called the play and told the guys the snap count. Then he took the snap and faded back into the pocket, stood in there as long as he could under a ferocious rush because Ben needed time to get across to the other side of the field before making his cut and flying up the sideline. Manorville seemed to bring everybody on the blitz except their two coaches.

Nate waited as long as he could before looking over to Ben's side of the field, saw him with a good two steps on the Rams' safety, and let the ball go right before somebody put him on his back.

There were at least two blue uniforms on top of him when he heard the cheer, what sounded like a home-field cheer even though he couldn't be sure. He managed to roll out from underneath the pile just in time to see Ben handing the ball to the ref at the 50-yard line, and saw the ref take the ball from him and then signal first down.

Malcolm was standing over Nate, reaching out with his hand to pull him up.

"What just happened?" Nate said.

"What just happened was this," Malcolm said. "Our quarterback put it just over the defender's outstretched hands, like the TV announcers say, put it over the defender and over Big Ben's outside shoulder, threw it about thirty-five yards on a dime before their safety got over and nudged our man out of bounds."

Malcolm tipped back his helmet so Nate could see the happy look on his face.

"Is all," Malcolm said. "Now let's go finish the bad dudes off."

They did. Nate didn't have to throw another pass, the game ending with the Patriots at the Manorville 5-yard line. Valley 14, Manorville 8.

Four days later, the day after the Brodie family received the FedEx'ed advance copy of the *Sports Illustrated* with Nate in it, the story about Nate ran on *Today*.

And at the end of it, after they'd shown the pass to Ben, after they'd shown the short interviews with Nate and his parents and Coach Rivers, the reporter showed the pass one last time, in slow motion.

As he did, Nate and his parents heard the reporter say this:

"Nate Brodie, the boy from a small town with the big arm. And maybe, just maybe, if dreams come true, a *million-dollar* arm."

Not anymore, Nate thought.

Not anymore.

CHAPTER 15

The Valley eighth-graders had the next Saturday off because of a conflict with the Valley High team. So they would be playing on Sunday afternoon this week, just like the pros.

At breakfast on Saturday, Nate's mom told him she had good news and bad news.

As soon as she did Nate said, "How many people?"

"Three couples, first one a little after two."

Nate nodded. She meant three couples would be looking at their house today. Which, *technically*, was good news, because it meant one of them or maybe even all of them might like the house enough to make an offer on it.

The bad news, for Nate, was strangers in the house. Strangers in the house *again*, even if they were the first strangers they'd had in a couple of weeks.

"Dad must be happy," Nate said.

His mom got up and went to get herself another cup of coffee. With her back to him she said, "As happy as he can be."

Nate's dad was already off to work at Big Bill's for a half shift today, one that would get him back home before the first couple arrived. Nate heard the car door slam a few minutes after he woke up. He went to the window and saw the red Big Bill's shirt behind the wheel of the Taurus as he backed out of the driveway, Nate still expecting to look out there and see the red Cherokee.

His dad had explained how important these "showings" were, making a sports analogy out of it for Nate, saying you never knew if today was the day that might change everything. Nate didn't care. He hated the showings, hated the idea of having to move, always made sure he found reasons to be out of the house when more strangers came walking through the front door. Moving through *his* world. Looking at *his* stuff.

The very worst was when he didn't have somewhere to go, Abby's or Malcolm's or Pete's or the library, anywhere besides 127 Spencer Street. And he would be in the house when one of the couples would bring along a boy or girl his age. Then it wasn't just having to put on a fake smile for the adults, but having to make fake conversation with a kid who might end up with Nate's room someday.

He didn't know how his dad, the real estate salesman, did it, acted as phony as he did with these people, trying to act as if they were the most interesting and important people in the world. Like there was no one else in the world he'd rather be spending time with.

Nate couldn't help himself—every time he knew his dad was

going to bring these potential buyers around, he put the Brady ball in a box in his closet. Sometimes he wanted his mom to take down all the stuff she was always taping to their refrigerator, photographs and notes and even the occasional clipping about Nate from the Valley paper, the *Advertiser*. Because that stuff wasn't meant for the eyes of people they didn't know. It was just meant for Nate and his parents.

Today his mom said, "I hope your room is clean, by the way."

Nate said, "Mom, if it's gonna take my room to seal the deal for Dad, we'll never sell this house."

When she turned around, Nate was relieved to see she was smiling.

"I don't expect it to look like a showroom," she said. "But I'd prefer if it didn't look like the twister in *The Wizard of Oz* just blew through it."

"I always hated that movie," he said. "Those flying monkeys still skeeve me out."

"But I think you get my point."

"Toto?" Nate said. "Toto, have *you* seen my football socks?"

"Socks off the floor would be a good start," she said. "Would, in fact, be *kickin'*."

Nate put his head down and said, "Please don't try to speak eighth grade. Or ninth . . . or tenth . . ."

"What's the matter?" she said. "That skeeve you out a little, too?"

The two of them had a laugh over that and Nate finished a

second stack of pancakes, told his mom he was going to ride his bike into town later and meet up with Pete and Malcolm so they could see the new Batman movie, and promised to do an official room check before he did.

"Haven't you guys seen it twice already?"

"Mom," Nate said. "It's *Batman*." As though that explained everything to her, not just about the movies, but about half the secrets of the universe.

"You should memorize school assignments the way you do dialogue from your superhero movies," she said. "By the way: Do you have any homework you could be working on?"

"Sort of," Nate said.

"Sort of?"

"Yeah," he said. "In fact, I think I'll go get on the computer and sort of start doing it right now."

"That sounds a little mysterious."

"Just trying to get smarter," Nate said.

"Always a good thing," she said.

Or maybe even a great thing.

Abby was always telling Nate that knowledge was power, and Nate hadn't been feeling powerful at all lately, on the football field or anywhere else.

He went upstairs and turned on his computer and got on the Internet and started looking for his own good news.

He stayed on the computer for a couple of hours, chasing one false lead after another, ending up feeling as if he were a dog chasing his own tail. But, he told himself, at least he was doing *something*, wasn't just sitting back. He was trying to make something happen the way he once did in games.

Even if it was just throwing one of those Hail Mary passes.

When he was finished, after he'd made his room look the way it used to when they still had a cleaning lady, he called Abby and asked if she'd changed her mind about going to the movies.

"I get a lot of things about you, Brady," she said. "*Most* things, actually. But the whole dark crusader thing you and the boys have got going for you, that I most definitely do *not* get."

"*Caped* crusader," he said. "*Dark* knight."

"Him too," Abby said.

Then she said that after he spent two and a half depressing hours with the dark caped guy, she'd meet him at Joe's for pizza and cheer him up.

Which is where they were now, Joe's, in their favorite booth in the front, having an early dinner. Between them was their usual, half pepperoni, half plain, and Abby was giving him a major pep talk about tomorrow's game against Ridgefield.

"You talk a much better game than I play right now," he said.

"Speaking of talking," she said, "there's something I need to tell you."

Nate saw that she had her serious eyes on. "What?" he said.

"I might be going away to school," Abby said.

Nate stopped eating then, felt a little bit as if he'd stopped breathing at the same time.

"Excuse me?"

"You heard me," she said. "I might, possibly, nothing final yet, still in what my folks say is the *discussion* stage, be going away for school second semester."

He was hearing her just fine, of course. Just didn't want to be.

"Where?" Nate said.

"This place where I'd feel a little less different," Abby said. "Where everybody can't see."

CHAPTER 16

The Perkins School for the Blind in Watertown, Massachusetts, was the most famous school of its kind in the world, according to Abby.

Nate just sat there in the booth like he was in the front row at school, listening to one of his teachers, listening to all these facts about Perkins, not touching the slice of pizza on the plate in front of him. He wasn't hungry all of a sudden, just trying to take it all in like it was some kind of class and if he missed something it might really, really cost him down the road.

"Helen Keller even went there for a while in the late eighteen hundreds," Abby said.

"Who's Helen Keller?"

"You know," Abby said. "Helen Keller from *The Miracle Worker*."

Nate put his hands out, shook his head, as if telling her: no clue, none.

Abby said, "She wasn't just the first famous blind person, she was deaf, too. She had this great teacher named Annie Sullivan, way before she went to Perkins. Helen Keller, I mean. Annie Sullivan was actually the one they called the miracle worker, for getting through to Helen Keller and finding out how brilliant she was even if nobody knew it back then. *And*"—Abby took a deep breath, the way his mom did sometimes in the middle of a speech about something—"to make a really long, interesting story short, Helen Keller ended up at Perkins and later on became a writer and speechmaker and political leader and had pretty much become one of the most admired women on the entire planet by the time she died."

She was trying to smile her way through this, giving Nate a crash course on the famous blind woman from the front booth at Joe's Pizza.

All Nate heard was this: Abby might be leaving.

"It's only a semester, Brady," she said. "Even if I do leave, it's not as if I'd be leaving you forever."

"But . . . you're not blind," he said.

"Yet."

"Okay," he said. "You're not blind *yet*."

"Listen, I know I could wait to start learning the stuff I need to learn," she said. "But we finally decided, or we're just about all the way decided, that the stuff I *could* learn at Perkins while I still can see, what they call 'life skills' there"—Abby put air quotes around the words—"would be easier than if I tried to learn them after the lights go out."

Making it sound like a switch somebody was going to throw. Nate thinking: And I'm worried about making a throw in football.

"Say something, Brady."

"I'm not smart enough to say the right thing. Or know what the right thing is."

"It'd be one semester," Abby said. "Think of it as if I was going off to boarding school and then coming back in time for summer."

"You make it sound like some kind of vacation," he said. "But I *am* smart enough to know it's not."

"Okay, it's not," she said. "So from now on we'll think of it as boot camp for blind people." She brightened then and said, "Hey! Maybe we could get somebody to do one of those TV series about me going to Perkins the way they do those dopey training-camp football shows you make me watch with you. What's it called?"

"*Hard Knocks,*" he said.

"*Hard Knocks,*" she said, "starring Miss Abby McCall. I could end up the new Miley Cyrus, just with ugly glasses."

"This isn't funny, Abs," Nate said, staring down at the table, shaking his head slowly, like he was hearing her just fine, but she wasn't hearing him. "Even you can't make it funny or seem like it's no big deal. I can't believe you didn't even tell me you were thinking about doing this."

She told him then that everything had happened kind of fast, that her parents were in constant contact with her teachers and that as "brilliant" as she was, Abby laughing when she said that part, she was having more and more difficulty keeping up, even with her handy dandy Mobile Reader.

"It's frustrating," she said. "And you know me, Brady. Even with these bum headlights, I still want to be perfect."

In a voice so quiet it was like it was coming from the back of the room, Nate said, "You already are, Abs."

Abby put her fingers to her lips then, reached across the table and touched Nate's cheek.

World's fastest kiss. If you blinked, you missed it.

"When?" Nate said. "When might you possibly, nothing final yet, be leaving?"

Feeling as if he were the one who'd been in the dark.

Abby took a deep breath and said, "This week."

Nate felt the breath come out of him now, like air coming out of a balloon.

But there was more.

"Actually," she said, "we leave tomorrow."

"Tomorrow?" Nate said.

"It's a trial week," she said. "My folks arranged it. So I can figure out if I'll like it there."

"*Tomorrow?*" Nate said, louder this time.

Abby said, "I know, I know, it means I gotta miss the game, Brady. But I can't help it, and besides . . ."

"I don't care about the stupid game!" he said. Now he was shouting, the words almost as loud as his fist banging on the table.

"Yeah, you do care," Abby said. "And so do I. But I gotta do this to find out if I *want* to do this, because it's pretty expensive."

As if money had ever mattered to the McCalls the way it did to the Brodies.

"I'll pay you *not* to go," he said.

"No, this is serious," she said. "It's *really* expensive."

She had overheard her parents the other night, she told Nate. "You know what kind of hearing I've got," she said.

Nate said, "Tell me about it."

"Anyway," she said, "I was supposed to be asleep but, like a lot of nights lately, I couldn't. Too many thoughts racing around my head, bumping up against each other like bumper cars. Good ones, bad ones, happy ones, sad ones. Things I've seen already. Things I might never see. That was when I heard Mom and Dad from down the hall."

Her mom was saying it was no problem, Abby could go to Perkins this year instead of the family going to Nantucket, to the house they'd always rented.

"My dad was angry, though," she said. "He said there was going to be no summer vacation this year, with or without Perkins, and that she knew it. Summer vacation wasn't the issue with Perkins, and she knew that, too. Then he started complaining about health insurance. I didn't understand half of what he was talking about, some of it was like a foreign language, but I was sort of able to figure it out. He was worried about how he'd be able to pay for it."

"*Your* dad was worried about paying for something?" Nate said.

Abby shrugged. Then she said, "But then he finished up by telling my mom he didn't care how much it cost, that I needed this."

Nate told Abby then about the night *he'd* overheard his parents talking about money, about how much they could use the million dollars and all that.

"We've both got pretty awesome parents," Abby said. "But I wonder sometimes if they'll ever figure out that they end up telling us important stuff without even knowing they're telling us."

Nate nodded, and for a minute neither one of them said anything. Joe's was starting to get more crowded, which meant the Valley High game was over. There was a Coldplay song coming out of Joe's old-fashioned jukebox. Nate heard a burst of laughter from the high school kids in the back room. Every so often the front door would open again and he would feel a quick blast of cold air.

Not as cold as the blast of air he'd gotten from Abby about the Perkins School for the Blind, though.

"So you're leaving tomorrow," he said.

"Think of it this way, Brady," she said. "Because I *can* still see, I'll be a total star at Perkins. The Nate Brodie of the whole place."

The Sunday *Boston Globe* was Nate's favorite paper of the week. He loved the sports section because it was full of stories about the Patriots, pages and pages of stats about their game that day and their opponent, and more pages after that about all the college football games played the day before.

Nate always woke up first on Sunday, never needing an alarm clock to get him up for church, always beating his parents to the *Globe*.

But when he opened the front door this morning, he found more than just the Sunday paper.

There was a present from Abby.

He figured it had to be some kind of painting or drawing because of its size and shape, wrapped in brown paper with a string around it. There was an envelope taped to the front that read simply, "Brady."

And Nate knew he'd better read the note or card or whatever it was first, imagining that Abby was spying on him to see if he did.

He didn't even wait to get inside.

The note said:

> Something to remember me by.
> And something to remember *you* by.
> Love,
> Abby Wonder

It was her new nickname for herself, in honor of Stevie Wonder.

When he was back inside, he dropped the Sunday paper on

the floor, because this was a day when the football stats and stories about the Patriots could wait. He lugged her present up the stairs, closed the door, and ripped off the wrapping paper.

Smiled.

Somehow she had drawn a perfect replica of the target he'd be throwing at in Gillette Stadium. The SportStuff logo was there, the hole cut in the middle.

Carrying it up the stairs, he had been surprised at how heavy the package was, and wasn't sure what it was made of even after giving it a rap with his knuckles. But it looked and felt and seemed as heavy as a stop sign.

In the corner, he saw, Abby had signed it and dated it.

The date was Thanksgiving night.

CHAPTER 17

It was one of those perfect football days.

One of those early-November days when it was cold but not too cold, the sun painting every part of the day as bright a color as possible: the navy blue road jerseys for the Patriots, the white home jerseys with the royal blue trim for the Melville Cowboys, the green grass, the orange of the leaves still in the trees that surrounded the field.

It was too good of a day to feel bad about anything, Nate thought, trying to give himself the kind of pep talk he knew Abby would have given him.

It's *football*, he told himself as he ran out on the field to start warming up with the guys.

It's not life or death or losing a job the way his dad had lost his, the way he knew dads all over the country were losing theirs. It wasn't being worried about losing your house or worrying about moving to a new house if you ever managed to sell your old one.

It sure wasn't losing your eyesight the way Abby was, or having to go off to a school for the blind where she wasn't going to know anybody, a school that Nate didn't think was going to make her feel less different.

She was Abby, after all. It meant that even with what vision she had left, she was going to see way too much, see way too clearly what her life was going to be like someday, how dark her world was going to become.

Come *on*. It was practically like he was shouting at himself inside his head. You put football up against all that and a morning like this should feel as good and exciting as Christmas morning.

Nate was doing his pregame stretching now, one leg out in front of him on the grass and then the other, and realized all over again that football was where you went to get away from bad news or bad thoughts. He looked across the field at Melville's own star quarterback, Danny Gilman, somebody he'd been going up against since he'd started playing football against other towns, and just knew Danny had to be feeling the same way on a day like this.

So Nate wasn't going to worry about the perfect throw he wanted to make on Thanksgiving night. Not today, at least. He was just going to worry about making solid throws against Melville. Even though Abby wasn't sitting up in the stands. Even though he knew she wouldn't be staring hard at him when he looked up there, believing she could get inside his head the way pro coaches did with those high-tech transmitters that sent plays in to the quarterbacks.

He was going to play today like this was the kind of priceless day they talked about in the credit-card commercials, the kind of day he'd pay anything for.

Even a million bucks, if he had it.

He started playing catch from twenty yards away with Eric Gaffney, did what he always did as he got into it, starting to feel himself humming the ball, motioning for Eric to keep backing up until he was forty yards away. Then Nate hit with him a spiral that should have given off sparks, Eric not having to move a single step to catch it.

Yeah, Nate thought, this was going to be the day when everything felt right for him and the team and the season, when they played like the team they were supposed to be, with the sure-armed quarterback they were supposed to have.

Coach Rivers always saved the best part of his own pep talk for last, a few minutes before they ran onto the field for the opening kickoff.

Sometimes it was about football, sometimes not.

Today he used baseball.

"I want you guys to go out there and have a Joe DiMaggio day," he said. He looked around at them and said, "Anybody happen to know who Mr. DiMaggio was?"

"One of the greatest baseball players of all time, for the Yankees," Nate said. He knew about all the great old Yankees because his dad had grown up in upstate New York as a Yankees fan, even if they were living in Red Sox country now. "He was a center fielder, he played in ten World Series in his career, and the Yankees won nine of them."

"Excellent!" Coach said. "Now here's what I mean about having a DiMaggio day. He played this game against the Browns near the end of his career—"

"The Cleveland Browns?" Eric said.

Coach smiled. "No, the St. Louis Browns. Who later became the Orioles. Anyway . . . somebody asked him after the game why he had played so hard against a lousy team even though the Yankees had already clinched the pennant, and Mr. DiMaggio said, 'Because there might be somebody in the stands today who'd never seen me play before, and might never see me again.'"

Coach let that sink in for a minute, even though Nate knew exactly what he meant, and hoped his teammates did, too. Sometimes the first impression you made on people was the only one you got, in sports or anything else.

"So go out there and have *that* kind of game against these guys," he said. "At the end of it have people think they just saw the best eighth-grade football team they're going to see all year."

Yeah, Nate thought.

Yeah.

Only it was Melville that looked that way and played that way on the first drive of the game. Danny Gilman threw on almost every down, to just about every one of his receivers, connecting with them all over the field. Not just confusing the guys on the Valley defense, but making them look a step slow for the first time all season, coming at the Patriots at Nascar speed. Danny's last pass of the drive was to his tight end, over the middle, wide open in the end zone after a play fake that fooled even Nate on the sideline.

Three minutes into the game and it was 7–0 for the home team.

"Okay, kid," Coach Rivers said to Nate. "Now we show these suckers what we've got."

Nate already knew the Patriots were coming out throwing today, having seen the first ten plays from the e-mail Coach had sent him the night before. Eight of them were passes.

But Nate hoped they'd only need the first one.

"We're throwing with both hands if we have to," Coach Rivers said. "Like your buds like to say, Number Twelve. Time to put your man suit back on."

The first play of the game was Nate's favorite from their play-book, a flea flicker they'd never before used to start a game. Nate handed off to LaDell, handed it to him as if it were a straight running play, LaDell running right up Malcolm Burnley's back side. Except one step before he got to the line of scrimmage, LaDell put the brakes on, same as his blockers did.

LaDell spun around then, pitched the ball back to Nate.

And as soon as the ball was back in Nate's hand, he didn't hesitate. Like a snap he'd taken in shotgun formation, he turned and looked to the right sideline, where he knew Pete Mullaney was going to be a streak of light, behind the defense already if the play had worked the way it was supposed to.

It had.

Like a charm.

Pete, Nate could see, had blown past the cornerback covering him. And the corner was getting no help from his strong safety, who'd pinched in as soon as he saw LaDell with the ball. Malcolm, meanwhile, had knocked over the Melville nose tackle like a bowling ball knocking over a pin.

Time to let the ball rip.

It wasn't the tight spiral Nate had thrown to Pete on his last warm-up toss, the ball wobbling a little in the air, but it didn't matter. Nate still managed to lead Pete perfectly. Pete gathered the ball in at midfield and ran away from everybody like he was trying to set a record in the fifty-yard dash. Just like that, one play, Valley was on the board, too.

Nate didn't chase Pete into the end zone the way he sometimes did, just ran straight over to the coaches to find out what play they wanted to run for the conversion. They would go for one point—a straight run with LaDell. Malcolm leveled their nose tackle again, LaDell fell across the goal line, and it was 7–7.

Nate wasn't thinking about having a Joe DiMaggio day now.

A Nate Brodie day would do him just fine, thank you very much.

I'm back, he thought.

Melville was an even smaller town than Valley, and it showed in the number of players on their team. By Nate's count of the players on the sideline plus the eleven on the field, they had a total of sixteen. So a bunch of their kids had to play both ways, offense and defense, including Danny Gilman, who on defense was playing the position of rover back. He was big enough to play like a linebacker when he wanted to, but still fast enough to drop back and be an extra safety on sure passing downs.

Basically he was free to rove the field like a one-man wrecking crew.

Danny had gotten fooled along with everybody else on the flea flicker to LaDell to start the game. But Nate was still tracking him on every play the way those Weather Channel guys tracked big storms, always making sure he knew where Danny was before Malcolm snapped him the ball.

But on the Patriots' fourth possession of the game, the score still 7–7, it was as if Danny was the one inside Nate's head, reading his mind, as if he knew *exactly* what Nate was going to do on a second-and-twenty play from midfield.

Danny stepped right in front of Eric on what was supposed to be a fairly nifty crossing pattern and intercepted the ball before Eric even got his hands all the way up. Then he broke to the outside like he was swimming against the whole flow of the play, and ran the rest of the way untouched for the score that put Melville back up a touchdown.

Nate thought he'd looked Danny off the second he got himself back in the pocket by eyeballing Pete, hard, on the left sideline, his eyes locked on Pete until he'd counted down in his head and knew it was the perfect time to deliver the ball to Eric, coming from the other side. And Nate thought he'd had plenty on the throw, like you always had to have when throwing over the middle. It didn't matter. Danny, using one of his own linebackers as cover, almost like a shield, was so perfectly positioned once the ball was in the air that it was as if he were part of the pattern himself. Like an *X* on one of Coach's play sheets had turned himself into an *O*.

Coach liked to tell him that football wasn't a game of one-on-one if you were a quarterback, it was one-on-eleven—all eleven guys on defense. But Nate felt like it had turned into one-on-one now because the other QB had just beaten him badly, like this had turned into basketball and Danny Gilman had just dunked on him, hard.

When he came off the field, Coach Hanratty got to him first.

"Dude," he said, "the guy's a total gangster. You're gonna have to know where he is on every play the rest of the game, or you gotta eat the ball."

"I've been trying," Nate said. "I thought I knew where he was on that play."

Coach Hanratty said, "You know my first rule of football. No medals for trying."

On the very next series, the Patriots back on offense, Danny came on a blitz along with what felt like the whole town of Melville, came from Nate's blind side, hitting him hard and clean and knocking the ball loose. One of the Cowboys' linebackers recovered it at the Valley 15-yard line.

Two plays later, after another Danny Gilman touchdown pass and successful conversion, Melville was ahead 21–7.

They were one series into the second quarter and Nate had already been intercepted once for a touchdown and practically fumbled away another touchdown, coughing up his own confidence at the same time.

Back? Yeah, he was back, all right.

Back to throwing the ball around as if he had a rag arm, back to missing wide-open guys, back to fretting over every single throw, whether it was into coverage or not, into Danny Gilman's area or not. He threw seven straight incompletions.

It wasn't quite a miracle that the game was still 21–7 at halftime, because there was no miraculous stuff going on with the Valley defense, who had stepped up their intensity and were playing as if every snap Danny Gilman ran and every series Melville had was the whole game. Sam Baum forced Danny to fumble one time and Malcolm personally separated their fullback from the ball another. And so the Patriots hung in there despite still being down two touchdowns.

When the half ended, Nate sprinted off the field, not even bothering to look up into the stands, knowing Abby wouldn't be there. Even his mom wasn't there today. She was doing volunteer work at the hospital.

Pete and Malcolm came and sat with him, one bud on either side, both holding a bottle of Gatorade. The day was cold enough that when they took their helmets off, Nate could see the steam coming off of them, though it really should have been coming out of their ears after the way Nate had played. Their uniforms were covered with dirt and grass stains and even what looked like a couple of small drops of blood, as if all the effort the two of them had made, the effort *all* the guys on defense had made, was painted on the fronts of their uniforms and told a story as brilliantly as Abby could have with one of her paintings.

Malcolm offered his bottle of Gatorade to Nate before he even unscrewed the cap. Nate shook his head.

"Don't try to make me feel better," he said.

"It's only Gatorade," Malcolm said, grinning, "not gold."

"I'm *killing* us," Nate said. "We're the ones who should be up two scores, not the other way around."

"Can I say one thing?" Pete said.

"No."

"You gotta stop acting as if it's on you to win the game all by yourself," Pete said. "Or think you're losing it all by yourself."

"If Danny Gilman was taking snaps from Malcolm instead of me," Nate said, "you know I'd be right about the score."

In a quiet voice, over the scratchy music being piped in over the loudspeakers at each end of the field, Malcolm said, "But he's *not* our quarterback. You are. We don't want him to be taking snaps from me. We want you."

"So just go play like you in the second half," Pete said. He grinned. "Problem solved!"

Malcolm stood up and said, "And stop whining or we'll tell Abby."

He knew they were right about all of it, especially the whining. He knew he wasn't going to reverse the slump he'd been in, *was* in, all at once. He couldn't tie up the game with one throw. It didn't work that way in football. Nate was going to have to get himself out of this one complete pass at a time.

But the throws kept missing their marks in the third quarter. The one that hurt the most was an incompletion he tossed over Eric's head when he was all alone in the back of the end zone on a fourth-down play that would have brought Valley back to within a touchdown.

The guys on defense continued to play like champs, though, continued to keep their team in it. They notched up their pass rush enough that suddenly Danny Gilman was missing his receivers as much as Nate was. So the game became a battle of field position, the way so many games did. But the problem for the Patriots was that even when they managed to get good field position, they weren't able to take advantage of it. It wasn't hard for Melville to figure out that Nate couldn't complete a pass to save his life today. So they kept putting more and more guys in the box to stop the run, daring Nate to throw.

So this was the same guy he'd been for weeks, unable to get out of his own way, his head filled with so many bad thoughts that he imagined a long line of them outside, waiting to get in.

Not a Joe DiMaggio day.

Groundhog Day was more like it.

Making the same mistakes over and over again.

Finally, at the end of the third quarter, the teams switching ends of the field, Coach Rivers came over and said to Nate, "We'll get you squared away in practice this week. But for the rest of today, let's give Eric a chance, see if he can get us going."

He'd been benched.

CHAPTER 18

Nate couldn't remember the last time he had been benched.

Couldn't remember if it had *ever* happened.

But now that it had happened, he wasn't surprised, or even angry.

For Eric, who had been taking a few snaps in practice each week as Nate's backup, it was as if he'd been waiting all season to get his chance to run the team. He completed his first four passes, the last one a total screaming ice-cold silver bullet to Pete, a thirty-yard touchdown pass that finished off a sixty-yard touchdown drive. Then he lofted a pass over Danny Gilman to Bradley Jacob for the conversion.

It was 21–14 now, and even standing on the sideline, Nate knew the momentum of the game had changed. You could almost feel it in the air.

A few minutes later the Patriots' free safety Sam (The Bomb) Baum picked off a Danny Gilman pass and returned the ball to the Melville 10-yard line. On the very next play, LaDell knocked over three different tacklers on his way into the end zone.

It was now 21–20 and the parents and family and friends

from Valley who'd made the trip to the game, sitting in the stands behind them, suddenly made it sound like a home game for the Patriots. Nate watched it all, heard it all, from next to Coach Hanratty, cheering like crazy with the rest of the guys on the sideline as LaDell ran in the conversion that tied the game at 21, but feeling at the same time that he should have been sitting in the stands where Abby and his mom usually sat.

It looked as if the game might end in a tie, but Valley forced Melville to punt with just under two minutes left. It was Eric's first chance at their two-minute offense.

He handled it like a complete pro, mixing short passes to the side and passes over the middle, calling two plays in the huddle when he had to, spiking the ball when he needed to, and finally advancing the ball inside the Melville 10-yard line with eight seconds left.

On first down LaDell caught a quick swing pass to Eric's right and looked like he might run it in, but Danny Gilman came out of nowhere, came flying across the field to knock him out of bounds. The clock stopped with three seconds left. Eric jogged over to talk with the coaches.

"I'm going with the lob pass to Bradley," Coach Hanratty said to Eric, "the one we got your conversion on."

"Love it," Eric said.

He ran back to the huddle, and Nate could see him pointing to the linemen as he told them the play. They lined up, with only LaDell behind Eric. Malcolm snapped Eric the ball. Nate watched as Eric calmly dropped back and lofted a floater into the air that was going to be the last play of the game, one way or another, watched as Bradley fought off two Melville defenders for the ball, getting it into his huge hands, hitting the ground so hard that it was like he'd fallen out of his bedroom window.

But he held on to the ball.

Came down with the ball and the game.

It was the throw to end the game that Nate had imagined, the perfect comeback he'd imagined.

Just not his.

He thought about going over to Coppo when Pete's parents dropped him off at home, but couldn't even picture himself picking up a football again until practice on Tuesday.

Strictly temporary, Coach had said about his benching.

Right, Nate thought.

Until it became strictly permanent.

Coach Rivers had said Nate would get squared up during the week. But how exactly was he going to square it up with the other guys on the team, guys who wanted to win the game and the league championship as much as Nate did? How was Coach going to explain to *them* that Nate was still the starter, no questions asked, after the way Eric had played against Melville?

It seemed like just the other day that he'd been worrying

about how his throwing was going to look on *The Today Show*. Now Nate was thinking how lucky he was that *Today* hadn't shown up to see him standing there next to the coaches at the end of the game and doing everything except carry one of those clipboards backup quarterbacks carried in the pros.

Watching the guy who was supposed to be his backup win the game.

His parents were watching the news on television when he came through the front door. Nate never knew what to expect these days from his dad, what kind of mood he would be in when he was around. He seemed to know this dad less and less.

Tonight, though, the old dad was back, his arm around his mom's shoulders, turning and giving him a big smile.

"How goes the battle?" he said.

Nate was already at the foot of the stairs, just wanting to get up to his room, close the door, be as alone as he'd felt when the game against Melville ended.

He almost said, "We lost," before he caught himself.

"Beat 'em on the last play of the game," he said.

"No kidding!" his dad said. "Pass play?"

"Yeah."

His dad said, "Who'd you throw it to—Pete?"

"I didn't . . ."

"Who was the lucky receiver then?"

"I didn't make the throw, Dad."

"But you said . . ."

"Eric threw it," Nate said. "To Bradley." His dad was still twisted around on the couch, looking confused now, still not getting it.

His mom was staring at Nate, too. She said, "Honey, did you get hurt, is that why you couldn't finish the game?"

"I got benched," Nate said, the words spilling out like change when you emptied out a pocket. "I played lousy, I got benched, Eric went in and threw the ball the way a good quarterback is supposed to and we came back from two touchdowns down and won."

He had started moving as he spoke, was halfway up the stairs now, like he was trying to escape a rush, trying to find some open field, this time behind a closed door.

His mom knocked on his door about seven thirty, carrying a plate with a burger and fries, saying she had just checked her parents' manual and that after a rough game you *were* allowed to have food in your room.

"Thanks," he said.

"Don't feel like talking?" she said.

"Nope."

"Never again?" He looked up to see her smiling at him and he smiled back, couldn't help himself despite feeling about as happy as a rock.

"Probably not."

"Thought so." She placed his plate on his desk, along with a bottle of Gatorade. "Your dad said to tell you that kickoff is in half an hour."

"Mom," he said. "Tell Dad I'm pretty much footballed out today. Even where the Pats are concerned."

"Forget about telling him," she said, still smiling. "For news like that, I'd better send out one of those Google alerts."

She left. He ate at his desk, managing to get through half the burger, not even touching the fries. When he was finished, he opened his laptop back up and went online, on the chance that Abby might be online at Perkins. Nate knew her well enough to know she must have brought her laptop with her.

She wasn't online, though.

But then, he thought, why should this part of his day be different from any other?

Nate found himself wondering what she was going through right now, this minute. Wondering if she had a roommate. What her room was like. What it was like learning to be blind.

Wondering how scared Abby was.

Man, Nate thought.

Man, man, man.

It wasn't just football that came out at you fast, it was *life* that did that.

He thought for a second about going down to watch the game, but this was a night when he didn't want to see the real

Brady do something great. He'd already seen one quarterback do that today.

So Nate went back to work online, back to places he'd bookmarked already, learning things he never thought he'd want to learn. Or *have* to learn.

Then the computer beeped. An IM.

Miss you Brady.

He nearly jumped out of his chair, banging his knee as he did, and typed out:

Not as much as I miss you.

But Abby was already gone.

CHAPTER 19

Tuesday, Nate's mom informed him that she had decided to take a second job.

She had been working four days a week—her workday always ending before Nate got home from school—at The Clairmont Shop in Valley. It was one of the businesses in town that had been around forever, a place that sold stationery and picture frames and plates and bowls and silverware, where women in Valley, Mass., could find nice things to decorate their houses or gardens or even their dinner tables.

Until she went to work at The Clairmont Shop, it was just another store on Main Street he'd been walking past his whole life. Or waiting outside if Abby was inside shopping for something, like a gift for her mom.

Now Nate's mom would also be hostessing at the American Grille, the best restaurant in town.

"You're gonna be a waitress?" Nate said.

"*Hostess*," she said. "Like a maitre d'."

"Whatever," Nate said. "But Mom, the Grille isn't a place you work at, it's a place we go to."

"It's only going to be for a couple of nights a week," she said. "You know the owner, Mr. Lopez, is a friend of your dad's and mine. He was in picking out a present for his wife at The Clairmont a couple of weeks ago, and when he saw that I was working there now, he said, 'If you wanted to go to work, you could've worked for me!' So I went in the other day and we decided to give it a try."

"When?" Nate said.

"Friday and Saturday nights to start, maybe throw in a couple of Sunday brunches for a while for good measure," she said. "No heavy lifting. Smiling nice at the customers, taking reservations, getting people seated."

"But that means you'll be working nearly seven days a week," Nate said.

She forced a smile, maybe practicing her hostess smile on Nate. "And Dad says math isn't your strong suit."

"You've gone from not working at all to working every day or night."

"Well, think how rested I am, not working all those years before this," she said.

They were sitting on the front stairs, side by side. It was where she'd been waiting for him when he'd come through the door.

Nate turned to her now and said, "We need the money that bad? Because now that I'm such a math whiz, I just figured out that you and Dad are working a total of four jobs between you."

"That is correct."

He was about to say that he never saw his dad anymore and now he wasn't going to see her, either. But Nate knew that wasn't what this particular talk was supposed to be about. It wasn't about him. So he didn't say anything right away. His dad had told him that sometimes the smartest thing in the world you could say was absolutely nothing.

"You okay with this?" his mom said.

"Do I have a choice?"

"Life's always about choices, sweetheart. Your dad and I are making some tough ones right now so that things will be better for our family down the road."

Nate said, "Will they?"

"You know me," she said. "I'm a silver-lining, blue-sky, glass-half-full girl." She put her arm around Nate, pulling him closer, Nate knowing she was trying to make him feel safe. "Always have been, always will be."

Nate said, "The only person I know with a better attitude than you—just slightly, like one of those photo finishes in the Olympics—is Abby."

His mom let out a big sigh. "Now, there's a change of subject I can handle," she said. "Just because ever being compared to Miss Abby McCall puts me in high cotton indeed."

"High cotton?" he said.

"It means I take it as high praise, young man," Sue Brodie said. "Which I do. How is your girl doing at Perkins, by the way?"

Nate stayed where he was, head against her shoulder now. It was something he could still do with his mom, but only when it was just the two of them like this.

"Haven't heard from her," he said. "Well, except for a hit-and-run IM the other night."

His mom said, "She must be pretty busy, a first week of school that's also her *only* week of school." She leaned back now so she could see Nate's face. "You miss her, don't you?"

"Yeah," Nate said. "But she's the one going through stuff, not me."

"Ha!" his mom said. "You're going through this right along with her."

"Not the same."

"You've got the biggest heart of anybody I know," she said. "So when somebody you love is going through stuff, so are you."

Nate gave her a look.

"Love?" he said.

She smiled again and said, "You got a better word for it, big boy?"

He wouldn't have touched that one even with one of his old fishing poles.

"Plus," his mom said, "it seems to me you're going through some *stuff* of your own with the Valley Patriots these days."

"We're not talking football today, all right?"

"All right it is."

Neither one of them moved. Nate could see from the big

standing grandfather clock in the foyer that there was still an hour before practice. It was amazing how quiet the house was in the middle of the afternoon, quiet and still, Nate able to hear the sound of his own breathing.

Finally he said, "You never ask me about making the throw anymore."

"Didn't know you wanted to give me updates."

"I just . . ." Maybe saying nothing would have worked for him again, but it was too late, he knew that, he could see the way his mom was looking at him.

She wasn't just a great talker.

She listened, too.

"What?" she said.

"Mom," he said. "You don't have to be a math whiz to know how much that money would mean to us."

"Wouldn't even think about trying to tell you it wouldn't, bud."

This was the first time they'd ever really talked about it. Not the adventure of it, not the excitement of it, not the chance to be on television or the chance to be famous. The money part. But the two of them were talking about it now, here at the bottom of the stairs.

"It would be great to have the million dollars," she said. "But whether you win it or not, it is still going to be one of the great nights of your whole life. Of our *family's* life. Which is why I don't want you to spend the next three weeks, or whatever it is, walking around with the weight of the world on your shoulders. Or thinking that you're going to be letting anybody down if you miss."

Nate nearly whispered as he said, *"I want to make it so bad."*

"I know you do." She lifted herself up a little bit so she could kiss him on top of his head. "But it's like I tell you all the time, about everything. All you can control is the process. Not the result. So enjoy the process and who knows? We might end up in fat city."

Fat chance, Nate thought.

He didn't say that to his mom, though, just told her it was time for him to start getting ready for practice, and went back up to his room. Then he pulled Abby's amazing replica of the SportStuff target from behind his chair, and propped it up against his desk.

He stared at the twenty-inch hole in the middle the way he did a lot these days.

He closed his eyes and imagined the ball going through clean and true on Thanksgiving night.

Imagined himself running over to wherever his parents and Abby were.

Tried to imagine—again—the roar of the crowd in Gillette Stadium.

Imagined the flashing lights of the cameras all around him, no matter which way he turned.

There was just one problem with the picture:

If he couldn't even throw as well as his backup quarterback, how was he going to throw one through that hole?

Coach Rivers pulled Nate aside before practice, asking him to take a walk with him, Nate thinking as he did that maybe everybody wanted to have a talk with him today.

Only he knew this one was going to be about *his* job, not his mom's.

"You know all about Bill Parcells, right?" Coach said. "Not everybody on this team is old enough to know what he did as a coach, but when it comes to football history, I know you're about as old as the ocean."

Coach, Nate knew, had his own way of getting to things. Getting into them.

"He came to the Patriots not too long after I was born," Nate said. "Drafted Drew Bledsoe and put us back in the Super Bowl. He'd already won two Super Bowls coaching the Giants."

"Just making sure."

"At least I can still deliver when it comes to history," Nate said.

"Hush and listen," Coach said. "Parcells wasn't just one of the greatest coaches of all time, he probably said more smart things about sports than anybody I know."

"'You are what your record says you are,'" Nate said, quoting him, not knowing where he'd heard that one from Parcells, just that he had.

"My favorite," Coach Rivers said. "But he said something just as smart once about quarterbacks. Said he didn't judge quarterbacks after they'd thrown three or four touchdown passes and won the game. He said that the real measure of a quarterback, for him and for the team, was after he'd thrown a bunch of interceptions and the crowd was booing and the media was after him and everybody wanted the backup to play."

They were leaning against one of the goalposts while the rest of the team started to warm up, one on either side. Now Coach leaned around so he was looking right at Nate. Grinning at him now. "You see where I'm going with this?" he said.

"I'd have to have my helmet on backward not to, Coach," Nate said.

"Parcells said that was when big players stepped up and showed what they were made of," Coach said. "I already know that about you." He pointed out at the other players. "Just make sure you show them, starting tonight."

And walked away.

Nate threw the ball in scrimmage much better than he had against Melville—after all, how could he *not*? He was still inconsistent, still didn't have his best control, still would see where he wanted to put the ball only to see it sail wide or high, or even bounce in front of a receiver.

But he hit Bradley one time in traffic, led him just enough and put the ball just high enough that only Bradley could catch the sucker. He floated one perfectly down the sideline to Ben and over Sam Baum, who was covering him, a ball that either Ben was going to catch or nobody was, at least not inbounds. He even cut loose with the best deep ball he had thrown lately, this one to Pete, straight fly, Pete reaching out as far as he could with his last stride at the 5-yard line, laying out, crossing the line. The rest of the guys on offense, led by Malcolm, actually applauded after that one. And Nate felt good enough about the throw, forty yards on a line, that he was able to joke about getting cheered for a practice pass.

"I don't want your pity," he said as Coach moved them back to midfield and told them to huddle up again.

"Wasn't pity," Malcolm said. "Shock, maybe."

"Shock and awe," Pete said.

Nate said to Pete, "Whoa, you mean you do pay attention in history sometimes?"

LaDell said, "Was a pretty fresh throw."

"It was Malcolm who said we should give you the standing O," Pete said, "on account of you really did look right-handed again."

Malcolm said, "See, there had been some conversation, just among us boys, that maybe you'd been a lefty trapped in a righty body all this time."

Nate smiled. "I think I liked your pity better," he said.

In this moment, just the normal give-and-take with the guys, Nate felt happy. Or relieved. Or both. Not just because he'd made the deep throw to Pete. Because he felt a part of it again, felt like he was really in the action again, even if it was just practice, not a spectator like he was at the end of the Melville game.

If practice had ended right there, with the pass and the chop-busting that came after it, Nate would have gone home happy. Only practice didn't end then. Nate ran one more series, got the offense into the end zone again with a short pass to a wide-open LaDell, and then Eric replaced him so he could get his reps with the first team.

And as Nate stood off to the side again, right next to the coaches the way he had been as Eric single-handedly beat Melville, he knew he was watching a different quarterback tonight.

He wasn't sure if anybody else on the field noticed it, at least with the exception of Coach Rivers, who somehow managed to see everything on the field, even with his back turned. But Nate sure noticed it, as if somebody had trained a spotlight on Eric Gaffney all of a sudden.

Eric was different because he knew he could do it now.

Knew *how*.

It wasn't anything he said or did. Wasn't anything the other players on the Valley offense said or did. But these weren't just end-of-practice reps now, Coach making sure Eric knew the plays and any new formations he'd thrown in just for fun. Eric was wearing the confidence of a real quarterback now like a shiny new badge, and Nate, who'd never been anything but, knew it better than anybody on the field.

Eric wasn't the starter, he was just playing like one. Throwing like one. *Acting* like one. Coming up to the line of scrimmage and moving Pete a little farther from the down linemen before he started calling signals. Turning and saying something to LaDell and Ben before another snap, switching off the play Nate knew had been called, faking the ball to LaDell and then keeping the ball himself and getting ten yards.

He didn't have any more arm than he had before the Melville game, it just seemed that way tonight, like he was a baseball pitcher who'd suddenly found a few extra miles per hour on his fastball. He ended practice with the same kind of two-minute drill he'd run in a real game two days before, finished up with a sweet throw to Ben in the corner of the end zone, Ben reaching up high and making a hands catch and still managing to keep his feet inbounds, dragging them like he was Randy Moss.

Then Eric ran over to Ben and bumped helmets with him like they'd won on the last play of the game all over again.

If you didn't know anything about the Valley Patriots, didn't know one player from another, were just sitting in the bleachers watching, you would have thought he *was* the starting QB, and maybe even the best player on the field.

You would have thought this was Eric's team.

CHAPTER 20

Abby called as soon as she got back from Perkins on Friday afternoon.

"Get over here, Brady," she said. *"Now."*

Nate hopped on his bike and raced to her house at Tour de France speed, glad that his mom hadn't seen how ridiculously excited he'd been on his way out the door.

Abby was in her art room when he got there, wearing the old sweatshirt she liked to wear when she was painting, the one so full of colors on the front and on the sleeves that it looked like she had lost several paintball wars. Badly.

"You had me break the world pedaling record to come over here and watch you work?" he said.

"Pretty much," she said.

"I guess it only took me one week to forget you're Multitask McCall," he said.

Abby smiled at him. "Oh," she said, "is that how long we've been apart. I *barely* noticed."

"Ha! You missed me *sooooo* much. Admit it."

It was the kind of thing he only said to Abby, and only when they were alone.

"Okay," she said in a soft voice, the one that came out of the place where he knew the truest Abby lived. "I admit it."

"But you're back now. That's all that matters."

"Matters for now."

"What's that supposed to mean?"

"It means I still might be going back for second semester," she said. "Or have you conveniently forgotten I told you that was a possibility at Joe's the day before I left?"

And Nate said, "Amazingly, no, I haven't forgotten. I was just hoping *you* might have."

"Well, we don't have to talk about that right now. I've got a few other balls in the air," she said, then told him about a visit she'd made to Children's Hospital Boston, to see one of their top eye doctors.

"Dr. Hunter is his name," she said. "Very cool guy, even not giving me the best news I've ever gotten."

"Like what?"

"Like if I'm going to be the world-famous thirteen-year-old artist Abby McCall, I'd better roll on that," she said.

"I have a feeling he didn't say it like that."

"Maybe not in those exact words," she said, her tone light and fun, as if they were discussing some must-see new You-Tube video. "He did tell me that my vision shouldn't be deteriorating this fast, not at my age. But it is, Brady. It just plain old is."

Nate's words came out hot and fast, the force of them surprising him. "There has to be something they can do to stop it!"

"They can't, Brady. It's why I've got to paint as fast as I can, whether I go back there or not."

She just let that settle then in the quiet room, like the dust Nate could see in the shafts of light coming through her blinds. He sat in his director's chair. His Nate chair. The easel she was working on was facing Abby. She didn't want him to see what she was working on, and he knew well enough not to ask. Her brushes and paints were on the floor around her. She went to work now, her face serious. Solemn almost.

After a few minutes, her hand moving in every direction at once, or so it seemed to Nate, she said, "This is my favorite place in the world. Especially when you're in it."

She could talk while she painted or sketched, had always been able to do that. And Nate had always loved listening to her. It wasn't like when he was alone with his mom and she talked just to talk sometimes, going on and on, eventually losing even Nate along the way. Making him want to get to the quiet of his room. Nate had never been afraid of quiet. He actually *liked* quiet.

It was why the guys on the team knew that when the game started, there was going to be only one voice in the huddle unless Nate asked somebody a question, and the voice was going to be his.

Yet the sound of Abby's voice never bothered him.

Never.

It was the absence of that voice that bothered him.

She was talking about Perkins again now. The more she did,

the more Nate could see something clear as day, like he could see forever:

The real reason she hadn't called him while she'd been away wasn't just because she was too busy. It was because she loved it there.

Loved being at a school for the blind.

This was her new world.

She needed it.

And Nate knew what *he* needed to do.

She finally took a break from painting and looked over at Nate. "So the last game stank, huh?"

"Like dirty laundry," he said.

"Still plenty of season left," she said. "You'll figure it all out before Thanksgiving night."

"You don't know that!"

His words came out hot, even made Abby jump a little, startled.

"Whoa," she said.

He took it down a couple of levels. "You *don't* know that," he said.

"I know you."

He took a deep breath.

Like he'd made a snap decision at the line to change the play.

Knowing it was the right thing to do.

"You know the me I used to be when it came to football," he said. "Not the player I've turned into. You probably hung around with guys at your new school who could throw more accurately than I can right now."

"Not funny."

"Not trying to be," he said. He took a deep breath, let it out, and kept going. "I'm just tired of people telling me that the season's going to work out fine, that everything is going to be the way it used to be. 'Cause it's not."

Then he quoted Parcells to her, telling her you are what your record says you are.

"Listen to me," she said.

Abby's voice was quiet, like she wanted the same from Nate. Like this room wasn't a place for loud voices or angry words and never would be.

"You know you don't really believe that," Abby said.

"See, that's what I mean," Nate said. "That's the thing. You think you know *every*thing about me, every single thought inside my head. And you don't."

He could see the hurt in her eyes. "I don't think that," she said.

"Yeah," he said, "you do."

He looked at her. "You don't always know me, Abs."

"No," she said. "I guess not." Her eyes were locked on his, Nate not knowing in this moment whether she looked more surprised or hurt at what had happened to her first afternoon back.

"Maybe I should just leave," he said finally.

"Maybe you should."

And he did.

CHAPTER 21

It was the first time he'd ever made it through a whole weekend, at least a weekend when he and Abby McCall were both in Valley, without calling her or talking to her online. Or seeing her.

Even though he wanted to.

At least there was a game for him to play and focus on, Saturday against Salisbury, a game the head coaches nearly called off because it was raining so hard. But because of the way the schedule was set up, there was no weekend the rest of the season when the two teams could play each other. So they played through the conditions, in what felt like the Mud Bowl game of all time.

Nate didn't have to worry about his throwing because it was almost impossible to throw in the wind and rain. He attempted two passes in the first half, two in the second half, handed off the ball more than ever to his running backs, and watched the two defenses slug it out. Finally, after the wet ball launched awkwardly from the Salisbury long-snapper to their punter, Nate cheered as Ben slipped from the outside to block a punt with four minutes left, then recover it in the end zone for a 6–0 Valley victory.

When it was over, Malcolm Burnley came over to Nate and said, "We are never going to be clean again."

Nate said, "I remember football in the mud being a lot more fun when we were little."

"Dude, are you joking?" Malcolm said. "We *won*. If that isn't fun, it's gonna have to do until something more fun comes along."

Nate thought about calling Abby when he got home, to tell her about the conditions at Salisbury, tell her what it was like trying to play football in what felt like quicksand. But he didn't. Didn't call her all day Sunday either, just spent part of the day on his computer and part of it at the library, feeling the way he assumed coaches had to feel when they were game-planning for the other team.

Looking for one opening that might change the game.

On Monday morning he and Abby sat next to each other on the bus the way they always did, acting as if nothing had changed between them, both of them knowing differently from the minute she sat down next to him.

He took a deep breath.

"Hey," he said.

"Hey yourself."

"Good weekend?"

"Yeah. You?"

"We beat Salisbury on Saturday in the storm. Ugliest game of all time. I kept expecting a cow to come flying across the field like in that movie *Twister*."

"How'd you do?"

"I didn't make any mistakes," he said. "For a change."

"Cool."

Normally she would have wanted to know all about it. Abby was always interested in the game even though she wasn't interested in football, interested in it because of Nate. It was the same way he felt about her painting: All paintings looked pretty much the same to him unless they were hers.

But things felt different today, not just on the bus.

At school, Abby sat in a front seat in every single classroom now, no matter where she'd been sitting before. And in Miss Buchanan's math class, their first class after lunch, her desk now had a small monitor that was like her own closed-circuit TV, Abby getting a close-up of the problems Miss Buchanan was writing out on the blackboard.

When math was over, Abby said to Nate, "This was one of the things they suggested at Perkins, and it turned out audiovisual was able to hook it up for me. You think it looked totally weird?"

"Nope. You know the deal with Miss Buchanan: The rest of us weren't even peeking at your desk. We have a hard enough time just getting it right at our own."

"It was either the monitor or wearing the glasses in class," Abby said.

"Which you hate."

"More than spinach," she said.

They were the last two in the room now, Miss Buchanan and everybody else having cleared out, Nate waiting for her out of force of habit. Abby was standing next to her desk and Nate was all the way in back, where he had always been in math.

It was when Abby started to walk back to him that she tripped over the leg of a chair that was sticking out in the aisle and went down.

Nate shoved his own desk out of the way to get to her, then hopped over a chair. But when he tried to help her up, she shook her head, no, and pulled herself up, like a fighter trying to bounce right back up after a knockdown.

It was when she was standing again that Nate saw the panic on Abby McCall's face, like the girl who couldn't even see the chair she'd tripped over had managed to see something else that scared her to death.

"You okay, Abs?" he said.

She didn't say anything right away, wasn't looking at him now, was looking over her shoulder, as if checking to see if it was still just the two of them in Miss Buchanan's classroom.

When she turned back around, she said, "Don't tell anybody, Brady. *Please*."

"Tell anybody what? That you tripped?"

"Just promise you won't," she said, the scared look still on her face. "Because if any of the teachers find out, they're supposed to tell my parents."

"Abs," he said, "you've fallen before, even at school. Then you do what you just did, which is get back up."

"I know. But I've been falling a *lot*." Her voice wasn't much more than a whisper now. "Even at Perkins. That's why they started teaching me to use a cane."

Nate knew what kind of cane she meant. Right away he pictured the blind people he would see in the street, cane out in front of them, tapping the sidewalk.

"They told me I should start using one at school, just to get used to it," she said.

Nate said, "But just a couple of weeks ago, we were at Coppo playing catch . . ."

He knew she had fallen that day, too, but in his mind he saw her before that, running on her long legs, running the way she used to.

Laughing her head off.

Being the Abby he still wanted her to be.

"It's been getting worse," she said. "I've been able to fake you out about how bad it's getting because I know you don't want to see it. Like you're the one with the bad eyes. You just see the stuff you want to. It's just . . . I can't fake myself out anymore."

"A cane," he said.

"They told me it was better for me to learn with it while I can still see. It will make it easier when I can't."

Nate thought she might cry then. The girl who never let him see her cry.

"I don't want to use a cane at school," she said. "It would make me feel like I was officially leading the freak parade."

"You know that isn't true."

"It would be worse than the glasses," she said. "Worse than that monitor, or the extra time they give me on tests now." She looked at Nate, somehow managed a small smile. "Worse than falling down."

"But when you got back from Perkins the other day," he said, "you acted like you were getting used to . . ." He put his hands out, like he was defenseless suddenly. "Getting used to the deal," he said.

"Getting used to going blind, Brady," she said. "It's okay, you can say it."

"You said you learned stuff there, how to be better at it."

"But I was *there*," she said. "Not here. There everybody was like me, or worse off than me, people who have been blind since they were born. Here they're not. Here I don't fit in anymore."

They just stood there now, a desk apart, Nate feeling as if that space were a canyon, knowing he had to say what they both were thinking before he lost his nerve.

"Maybe you need to be there," he said.

Abby didn't say anything. He thought she was about to, but she didn't, and she didn't cry.

She just closed her eyes and nodded.

CHAPTER 22

Game day.

Valley Patriots versus the Whitesboro Panthers.

The opening drive for the Patriots took seven minutes off the clock, an eighty-yard drive that resulted in a 7–0 lead. They mixed short passes and runs, most of the passes coming on first down, Coach Rivers and Coach Hanratty having decided they were going to use their passing game to set up their running game today, the way the pros did with the West Coast offense.

Nate had told them he was *so* down with that.

It was one of the best things about playing on this team, every game plan being different, no Saturday being anything like the one before it.

And it had worked. Nate had managed to complete all five of his passes on the drive, even though those five completions had gone for a total of only thirty yards.

Coming off the field Malcolm said, "You brought your good mojo today."

Nate said, "*You* could have completed those passes."

Malcolm gave him a playful shove and said, "Dude, what is it with you these days? I want to talk about mojo, you want to go looking for a dark dang cloud."

"I'm good," Nate said, and from behind him he heard LaDell say, "We gonna move those chains all day long, baby."

"All day," Nate said, wishing he believed it as much as his tailback did.

The Panthers didn't take long to respond, scoring on their second play from scrimmage, a sixty-yard pass-and-run play to their tight end. Just like that, the game was tied.

For some reason the Panthers doing it that easily, and that quickly, rocked Nate. He didn't want to get into a scoring contest and it showed. He threw his next pass over Ben's head and right into the hands of the Panthers' free safety.

Four running plays later, it was 14–7, Whitesboro.

On Valley's next drive, Nate hung a short out pass to Pete like a pitcher hanging a breaking ball. This time a Panthers cornerback stepped in, said thank you very much, went down the sideline so fast it was as if he had IM'ed himself into the end zone. Now it was 21–7, Whitesboro.

The next drive for the Patriots started off well enough. They went back to their version of the West Coast, strung together some first downs, got across midfield. But on the next play, a big pass rush in his face, Nate tried to force a pass to Bradley over the middle. The ball was way behind Bradley, bounced off the hands of the linebacker closest to him, and ended up in the hands of the free safety again. If Nate hadn't managed to catch the guy from behind, it would have been 28–7 at halftime, game over.

When he got to the sidelines, Coach Rivers put an arm around his shoulders and said, "We maybe could have thought about eating that one."

Nate pulled away, slapped the sides of his helmet, hard, with both hands and said, "I *know*, Coach. Believe me, I know."

"Sometimes the best throw," Coach said, "is the one you don't make," sounding like his dad telling him in a nice way that he should always know when to shut up.

Nate got one more chance to move the chains before halftime. Staying on the ground now, the Patriots drove down to the Whitesboro 20-yard line and were facing a second-and-five, half minute left. Nate looked over to Coach Hanratty's play board and picked up his hot read, a crossing pattern to Pete that was drawn up to have him open as he cut in front of the goalposts.

It was Pete's favorite route, and one of Nate's favorite throws to make, to his favorite receiver.

He went to a quick count, dropped back into the pocket, looked off the free safety by giving a long look at Eric, who'd run a quick little buttonhook move in the left flat. When he looked back to the middle, he saw that Pete had gotten his inside shoulder on the cornerback and had him by two strides, easy.

Had him cold.

Yet Nate couldn't pull the trigger.

He was afraid he might get picked off again.

It was the worst kind of fear there was in sports, the kind where you didn't give yourself a chance to do something right—even something great—because you were terrified you might do something wrong. So Nate didn't do anything. This time he ate the ball, for all the wrong reasons, got himself righteously sacked. Then got sacked again on third down when there was nobody open and nowhere for him to run. Coach Hanratty didn't even have him try a throw on the last play of the half, just had him hand the ball off to LaDell and run out the last few seconds.

When he got to the sideline this time, Nate knew what was coming, just by the look on Coach Rivers' face.

"We're better than those other guys," Coach said to him, taking off his Patriots cap, running a hand through his short hair. "And I owe it to the guys on our team to give us our best chance."

"Eric," Nate said quietly.

"Yeah," Coach said. "Sorry."

"I'd do the same," Nate said. "Really, I would."

"Be ready if I need you to go back in," Coach Rivers said before he walked away.

"You won't," Nate said, not sure whether Coach heard him or not.

He didn't stand next to Coach Rivers or Coach Hanratty the second half, just found himself a patch of grass about twenty yards away from them and stayed right there. Watched from there as Eric brought the Patriots back again, Nate *knowing* he was going to bring them back, knowing at the same time that Eric winning the Whitesboro game this way—which he finally did, 28–21—was the beginning of Nate officially losing his job.

When he got home an hour later, he found out his job wasn't the only one that had been lost that day. His dad had been laid off from Big Bill's.

CHAPTER 23

They were at the kitchen table. As soon as Nate walked in, he knew it was bad, the way you always did with your parents. Not *how* bad. Just bad. Just by the way they were looking at each other.

It wasn't just his mom's face, eyes red, obviously from crying. It wasn't just the look on his dad's face, the way he seemed to be staring past Nate's mom at some point over on the other side of the street. Or the other side of town. Or the world. It was the air in the room, thick and heavy, the way the air outside felt right before a storm was about to hit.

"What happened?" Nate asked.

It was his mom who said the words, his dad still just sitting there, staring off into space.

When his dad finally spoke, he said, "They told me they hated to do it. Said it had nothing to do with my job performance, said I was one of the best managers they'd ever had. But they had to cut costs. And I was obviously overqualified for the job in the first place."

Nate didn't move, stayed right where he was in the doorway,

uniform still on, helmet in his right hand. He looked at his mom now, thinking, You never cry. You never cry the way Abby never cries.

His blue-sky, glass-half-full mom, staring at him with red, sad eyes. "No warning," she said, "none," as if she were talking to herself.

Nate noticed that his dad was still in his Big Bill's shirt, the shirt Nate knew he hated, the one he usually couldn't wait to take off as soon as he got home from work. Only now maybe he didn't want to take it off because as soon as he did, then it became final, official, that he was out of a job. Again.

"What does this mean?" Nate said, knowing the question came out sounding stupid, but not knowing a better way to ask it.

Now his parents really were back to looking at each other, like they were waiting to see who'd make the first move. For a moment neither one of them spoke.

Finally his dad said, "It *means*, son, that I have to find another job."

"What kind of job?"

His dad blew out some air and said, "Any kind of job."

"Before . . ." Nate stopped himself, shifting his weight from one foot to the other. "Even before this," he said, "I heard you and Mom saying we might lose our house before we even got to sell it."

"I'm not going to lie to you, son," his dad said. "That's a possibility. Has been for a while. The way it is with a lot of other people right now. It's why I have to go back into the want ads tomorrow and see if I can find a job as soon as possible." He smiled, almost like he was making fun of himself, before he said, "Another dream job."

"But what if you don't, Dad? What happens to us if you *don't* find something right away?"

Nate's dad gave him a long look, then his eyes shifted back to Nate's mom. Then back to Nate. His dad shrugged. "Then we will lose this house," he said.

He slammed his hands on the table, stood up, said, "We'll lose everything," and walked out of the room.

Then Nate and his mom heard the front door open and close, heard the Taurus backing out of their driveway, followed by a brief screech of tires before the sound of the car disappeared up the street. The street Nate had grown up on, the only one he'd ever known.

Nate told his mom what had happened as quickly as he could, then went upstairs, got out of his uniform even more quickly, took a shower, and went into his room and closed the door.

Before he'd left the kitchen, his mom had told him she'd call him when it was time for dinner, that she had a feeling it was going to be just the two of them. Again.

"I'm glad I'm not working tonight at the restaurant," she'd said.

"Me too," Nate had said.

When he plopped down on his bed, he realized he was more tired from watching Eric win the game than if he'd won the game himself, as if he'd been the one making the passes and the plays, scrambling for first downs, throwing on the run, getting hit and getting back up. Nate realized as he replayed the game in his head—Eric's game—that he didn't just miss having the ball and the game in his hands, he even missed getting hit.

Nate missed the feeling that he would have after he'd played the whole game, not just a good kind of tired but a good kind of soreness, the normal aches and pains that were another way of knowing that you'd played your heart out.

Today he hurt in a different way.

He got up off the bed now, took the Brady ball out of its case, got back on the bed, stretched out, and began flipping the ball toward the ceiling and catching it. Loving that the ball still had that shiny, new-ball feel to it, even the smell of a new ball when you took it out of the box. Like a new baseball glove.

Nate thought about Tom Brady now, knowing he hadn't exactly had an easy time of it before he became—in Nate's opinion at least—the best quarterback in football and maybe the greatest of all time. Brady hadn't been a big star coming out of college. The Patriots hadn't even drafted him until the sixth round. And there had been that time, between college and his getting the starting job with the Patriots after Drew Bledsoe got hurt, when he really was nothing more than a practice quarterback pretty much everybody except his own teammates had forgotten, when he had to wonder if he'd ever get the chance to show the world how good he really was.

If he even knew how good he really was.

Even after he got the job and won three Super Bowls in four years, it wasn't as if Brady was bulletproof, not by a long shot. There was the year when the Patriots were going for a perfect season, when they were 19–0 going into the Super Bowl, and Brady had thrown fifty—five-oh—touchdown passes during the regular season. He was having the best season any quarterback in history had ever had and the Patriots were on their way to being called the greatest team of all time.

Until the Giants upset them in the Super Bowl, beat them in the last minute when the other quarterback in the game, Eli Manning, threw a touchdown pass. Good-bye, perfect season.

The very next year, in the first game of the season, only eight minutes of game time into the new season, a guy from the Kansas City Chiefs rolled into Tom Brady's left knee and ripped it up about every way you could, and just like that, Brady's season was over and his career was in jeopardy.

So it wasn't as if his hero hadn't been knocked down. Anybody could get knocked down. Anybody and everybody. It was like Bill Parcells had talked about: It wasn't how you got knocked down, it was how you got back up.

Corny-sounding, but true.

He kept thinking about Brady as he flipped the ball at the ceiling, thinking about how much he must have wanted to show the world all over again after losing the Super Bowl to the Giants, only to have to wait longer to try than he ever thought he would when he went down against the Chiefs.

Nate told himself: I don't have to wait.

I can do this now.

So he did. He put the Brady ball back in its case, pulled out Abby's SportStuff target from behind his reading chair, yelled down to his mom and asked her if she had time to help him with something.

"Always," she said from the bottom of the stairs. "What's our project?"

Nate opened his door, carrying the target.

"Hanging a dream catcher," he said.

Nate knew there had been at least one other who had made the kind of throw he was going to attempt on Thanksgiving night, because he had looked it up on the Internet and found the clip on YouTube where an Army veteran named Chris Bostic had won a million dollars at halftime of a Clemson–Florida State college football game.

Chris Bostic's throw had been sponsored by a company called Bi-Lo Healthy Choice, and the contest was called the Pigskin Challenge. This was in November 2005, and Bostic had to put the football through a twenty-inch hole from twenty-five yards away.

Nate knew how it came out because he had watched it enough by now, but he showed it to his mom, both of them watching on Nate's laptop as Bostic—whom the announcers described as not just a veteran and a former high school football player, but a "ten-dollar-an-hour landscaper" as well—stepped up as calmly as if he were ringing a doorbell and threw a perfect spiral through the target.

And the crowd roared.

When the clip ended, Sue Brodie said, "You've got better form than he does, and a better arm, let me just start off by saying that."

"Mom," Nate said, "that's not why I showed this to you."

"I'm just saying," she said, "that if *that* guy, and I'm sure he's a very nice and deserving person, can make a throw like that, *my* guy can do it, too."

"*Mom*," Nate said, "focus on the target. Please."

"Now I'm confused," she said, smiling. "Isn't it you who's supposed to be focusing on the target?"

He smiled back, thinking, At least we're not talking about jobs or money for a few minutes.

Suddenly it felt like a whole different day.

"You're being silly," Nate said.

"I am," she said. "And I can't tell you how good silly feels right now."

Nate said, "I want you to focus on the target so we can figure out how to set up mine in the backyard."

Then she told him to play the clip again, saw how the target was on a stand, said "piece of cake" and told Nate to follow her down to the garage and to bring the target.

When they got down there, Sue Brodie moved her and Nate's bikes and his dad's golf clubs out of the way and said, "Aha!"

Leaning against the wall, completely forgotten, at least by Nate, was the old pitch-back he and his dad had bought the year Nate was ready for Little League baseball. The one Nate had worn out that first spring when he wanted to pitch and neither his mom nor his dad was around to catch for him.

He couldn't remember the last time he'd used it.

"Let me have the target for a sec," his mom said, then held it up against the netting of the pitch-back and said to Nate, "Fits like a glove."

She was right. If you forgot what was behind Abby's target, it looked pretty much like the one Chris Bostic had thrown to.

His mom said, "Are you ever again going to need this contraption to improve your pitching skills?"

"Not likely," Nate said.

"Well, then," she said, "let's turn this into a dream catcher. Though technically, of course, we don't want it to *catch* your dream, we only catch the dream if the ball zips right through the hole, clean as a whistle."

She went into the kitchen, came back with the strongest ball of string she could find, and a pair of scissors. Then they lugged the target and the pitch-back into the backyard, far end, and she went to work, as serious about this job as if it were the job that was going to solve all the family's problems.

When she was finished, clearly proud of her handiwork, she stepped back and said to Nate, "Get a ball."

He ran inside and came back with one of his old practice balls.

"Okay, then," his mom said, hands on hips, as if she'd turned into his coach. "I would like you to step back . . . how far will it be at the Patriots game?"

"Thirty yards, five farther away than the guy on YouTube."

"Thirty yards it is," his mom said. "And then I would like you to miss."

"Miss?"

"I want you to hit anywhere around the outside of the opening," she said, "just to see if this sucker can absorb a hard hit."

"I've been throwing like a scrub," Nate said. "Missing the target I can do."

"Hush and do as you're told," she said.

Nate paced off the distance, rotated his arm a few times, windmill style, backward and forward, just to loosen his shoulder up. He took a deep breath and cut loose at Abby's target, not really caring where the ball went, not worrying about that big hole cut into "SportStuff."

The ball went through the hole as easily as if Nate had put it through the tire at Coppo Field.

"I thought I told you to miss," his mom said.

"I was *trying* to," Nate said, laughing. "I *wasn't* trying to throw a strike."

"Maybe we're on to something," his mom said.

"Funny."

"Well, could you please try—or not try—again?"

She tossed him the ball.

Nate put it through the hole again.

"Looks like we're going to be here awhile," Sue Brodie said, and retrieved the ball again.

On Nate's third try, he rattled one off the white space above "SportStuff," the ball making a big noise. But the pitch-back stayed standing.

"My work here is done," his mom said. "Have at it."

Nate did, until it was too dark and his mom was calling him in for dinner. Just him and the ball and the dream catcher that wasn't a catcher at all.

And for this one night, the less he cared, the more he made.

CHAPTER 24

Coach Rivers made it official before the start of Tuesday night's practice: He told the team that Eric would be starting against Westboro on Saturday.

He had told Nate before he told the rest of the team, Nate seeing how difficult it was for him. But Nate made it easy, telling him that he knew it was coming and that they both knew it was the right thing for the team.

"I'm trying to make you feel better about this and you end up making *me* feel better," Coach said. "Now how does *that* work?"

"I'm still thinking right along with you," Nate said. "I'll just be standing next to you."

"No," Coach said. "I want you on the field. I've been thinking a lot about that. You're too good of an athlete to stand on the sidelines. You're going to play some running back, probably more wide receiver. I might even take Bradley out and line you up at tight end once in a while. It'll drive the other coaches crazy, at least the ones who know who you are, have them thinking I've got something up my sleeve. I'm even gonna put in some direct snap plays to you, when you line up in the backfield with Eric."

Nate had stopped listening about halfway through. "You mean the coaches who *used* to know me," he said.

"I'm the one who knows you, inside and out. And if I'm half the coach you seem to think I am, I'm gonna get your throwing straightened out before this season is over."

That was when he and Coach walked out to midfield and everybody gathered around them and Coach told the team they were fortunate enough to have two quarterbacks they could win with, but that Eric had earned the right to start against Westboro.

Eric took a step forward then.

"Coach," he said, "you don't have to do this because of me. This isn't something I was ever looking for. I tell Nate all the time it's his team—"

Nate answered before Coach Rivers did. "No, it's not just my team. It's yours. And Malcolm's. And Bradley's. And Pete's. It's all of ours. Coach is always telling us how sports is a merit system. The best guys play. The best team wins, at least most of the time. Even if this wasn't a competition, you won the job fair and square, dude. So don't worry about me. Worry about Westboro, and just keep throwing the way you have been."

He bumped Eric some fist then, as Coach said there was really nothing for him to say because Nate had said it all.

From the time Nate had started playing sports, he had heard the expression "taking one for the team." He knew it came from baseball, the idea that you had to be willing to get hit by a pitch if that's what it meant to get on base and help your team win a game. And Nate knew how much it hurt to get hit by a pitch, even in Little League, because everybody did.

This had hurt more, saying what he'd said.

But Nate knew he was doing what the quarterback of the team was supposed to do.

Even if he wasn't the quarterback anymore.

Malcolm tried to pull him aside a couple of times during practice, telling him to hang in there. Nate saying, he got that, he really did.

"Now I get to hang in there at wide receiver," he said. "I can do that."

He was a good wideout, as it turned out. He knew the patterns better than the regulars did, knew what he liked when he was the one doing the throwing, knowing that the key was being exactly where the quarterback expected you to be.

By the time they were halfway through practice, Coach Rivers had him in there a lot. And Coach Hanratty, who called most of the plays even on the practice field, was making sure that Eric was throwing as many balls Nate's way as he was to Pete or Bradley.

He didn't get open every time. But he got open a lot. And

when he could get his hands on the ball, he caught it every time, challenging himself not to let a single ball hit the ground if it was anywhere near him.

The funny part?

He was working so hard at being a wide receiver and doing well at it that he felt more like a part of the team than he had for a while, whether he was out of position or not.

Pete's mom dropped him off at home when practice was over. Nate's mom was working tonight, had told him before school that one of the other hostesses at the American Grille was close to having a baby and was going off on what his mom called "maternity leave."

"Which means a lot more hours for me," his mom had said.

"How many more hours?" Nate had said.

His mom had smiled across the breakfast table, like she was about to deliver the best possible news in the world, looking like she did when she would wake Nate up with the two most beautiful words in the English language: "Snow day."

"Pretty much as many as I can handle," she had said. Then she'd reached across the table and put her hand over Nate's. "Just till we're back on our feet."

So Nate's dad was the one in the kitchen when he got home, banging around pots and pans, which made Nate smile. His dad cooking dinner was never a good thing, even when it was something as simple as pasta, which he was clearly preparing now.

His dad turned around when he heard Nate, held up two boxes of pasta.

"Fat or skinny?" he said.

"Angel hair." Nate's favorite.

"What about a salad?"

"Dad," Nate said, "you know you'd rather pull one of your teeth out with pliers than make a salad."

"Excellent point."

Nate said, "Do I have time to take a shower?"

"Please do," his dad said, "so you can just experience the result without watching the whole ugly process."

"Dad," Nate said, "do you want me to help you boil the water?"

"Go. Now."

When Nate came back down, he saw the open newspaper next to him, a lot of red circles on the want-ads page.

"Any luck today?" Nate said as they both started to eat.

"Little bit. Got a couple of interviews tomorrow."

Nate went to work on his pasta, which was surprisingly good.

"I can do this," his dad said.

"I know."

"We're not the only family this is happening to," his dad said. "I have a feeling there are lots of families in this town going through the same thing and we don't even know it. They'll get through it, and so will we. We've just got to hang in there."

Sounding like Malcolm at practice. Just talking about real life now, not football.

Nate kept eating, even asking for seconds. And his dad kept talking, almost as if he were talking to himself.

"It's just a question of attitude," he said. "Definitely. The guy who was going to Big Bill's every day, that guy wasn't me. You can't hate what you're doing, even if you're doing it for the right reasons. The *best* reasons. So now it's a matter of selling just one house I've got out there, which would change everything. Or finding the right fit doing something else, finding something I *want* to do even if it turns out to be something I never thought I'd be doing."

Now Nate looked up, grinning, and said, "Like your son, the wide receiver?"

"He made Eric quarterback?"

"I gave him no choice, Dad, the way I was playing. Coach had to do it."

"But even the best quarterbacks go through slumps."

"Sometimes it's more than a bad slump, it's just a bad season."

"Yeah," his dad said. "For everybody." He shook his head and said, "I'm sorry, pal."

"You didn't do anything."

"Other than acting like a jerk lately," he said. "Or just a stranger.

I'm sorry about that, sorry this has happened to our family, sorry your mom is holding down two full-time jobs now."

"I don't worry about you," Nate said. "You've always taken care of us."

"Till now."

Now Nate was smiling. "Until we're back on our feet."

"Yeah. Until then."

Nate put his fork down. "Are we going to lose our house, Dad? Really?"

His dad gave him a long look. "I hope not," he said. Then he got up suddenly and did something he hadn't done in a long time, pulled Nate out of his chair and hugged him and told him not to stop believing in happy endings, no matter what, no matter how hard that was sometimes.

Nate went upstairs and made himself do all of his homework, even some stuff for Friday's math quiz that he could have put off for a night. Made himself do his homework before he checked his e-mail or even thought about IM'ing any of his buddies.

Or Abby.

He hadn't been talking to her much lately, as difficult as that was for him, making him feel as if it wasn't just his mom who wasn't there for him right now—it was Abby, too. But he thought he might make an exception tonight because Abby hadn't been at school today and nobody was sure why, not even their teachers.

It was when he went online that he saw the Google Alert he'd set up for himself.

Clicked on the link Google had sent to him.

Read the story.

Then read it again to make sure he understood it.

Then he printed it out and waited.

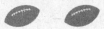

When his mom came home, Nate was sitting at the bottom of the stairs, printout in his hand. It was a few minutes after eleven, which meant way past Nate's bedtime. Even his dad was fast asleep upstairs.

"Good," his mom said. "You've printed out your explanation for why you're up this late. Very official."

Nate motioned for her to sit next to him.

"Been waiting for you," he said.

"And whatever you've been waiting for me *for*," she asked, "cannot wait until morning, when I have rejoined the ranks of the living and functioning?"

"No," Nate said. "It can't."

She sat down and Nate handed her the printout. She read it. When she was finished, Nate explained why it was so important to them, and why she had to take him to Boston as soon as she could fit it in around her work schedule.

Nate said they had to do it even if he had to miss a day of school, and a practice.

"Mom," he said, "this could change *everything*."

She smiled. "This is the top secret project you've been working on?"

"My game-changer. Maybe."

"The kind your dad is always talking about," she said.

Now she was the one hugging Nate, on this night of hugs. Then she said, "A lot has changed around here, kiddo. A *whole* lot. But one thing sure hasn't."

"What's that?"

"You're still leading with your heart."

CHAPTER 25

This is the way Abby had explained her absence from school when she'd showed up on the bus Tuesday morning, wearing her special glasses to school for the first time:

"Had a bad day, is all."

Nate knew the bad days were going to start coming more frequently.

The distance between them was still there. This was the new Nate-and-Abby, the world the two of them were living in now.

He wanted to talk about stuff the way they used to, talk about everything under the sun, make things the way they used to be. But he told himself that wasn't going to do her any good.

It was Nate's turn to miss school on Wednesday. He and his mom had raced up to Boston for the meeting she'd been able to set up.

Then Abby missed school again on Thursday. It was becoming routine now, routine for the two of them not to see each other or even speak to each other. When Nate arrived home Thursday from school, the package he'd forgotten he'd even ordered was waiting for him. And this time, he ignored what his head had been telling him and he led with his heart again.

He rode over to Abby's on his bike, didn't ring the doorbell, just left the package on her doorstep the way she'd left him the SportStuff target that day. Then he turned right around and went home.

There was no football practice on Thursday night this week, nothing until the Westboro game on Saturday. His dad, Nate knew, was on his way back to Valley from another job interview about an hour away. His mom was at The Clairmont Shop. So Nate was alone in the quiet, empty house, not bothered by that anymore, getting used to being alone. He used the quiet time to get his homework done, wanting to watch the Thursday night game on the NFL network between the Packers and the Jets.

He had just finished the chapter they were going to be quizzed on in history tomorrow when the phone rang.

Nate looked at the caller ID and smiled.

"You think you can just drop this off and run home like a weasel, you weasel?" Abby said.

"I think two *weasels* is a little strong," Nate said.

"Get over here, Brady," Abby said. *"Now."*

The book was called *The Story of My Life* by Helen Keller, and Nate had gone looking for it on the Internet after Abby had told him about Helen Keller that day at Joe's Pizza.

It was Keller's autobiography, described as a "restored classic" on Amazon, and Nate couldn't believe there was an audiobook version of it. But there was.

There was a long review of the book posted on Amazon, and the guy writing it started by saying how "Helen Keller would not be bound by conditions," and down near the end he quoted from the book: "There were barriers, it is true," she wrote. "But barriers that could in time be swept away."

The review ended with a sentence about how this blind, deaf woman opened people's eyes and ears to the beauty of the world. When Nate got to that part, he realized it was like the guy was writing about Abby. He'd ordered the audiobook right there and then.

So much had happened since then, from Abby going to Perkins to Nate losing his starting job to his mom adding a job and his dad losing *his*, that Nate really had forgotten about the audiobook until it arrived.

When he got to Abby's house, her mom told Nate she was waiting for him upstairs in her studio. And when he got up there, the first thing he noticed was that all the paintings she'd been working on the last time he was here were now covered.

Abby wasn't wearing her glasses today, maybe because the shades were drawn, most of the light gone from the room, making it look and feel as if it were already night outside.

She had the box for *The Story of My Life* in her lap.

"Why'd you have to give me this?" she said.

"Uh, because I thought you'd like it?" he said. He smiled at her and said, "I know that sounds like an epically terrible reason . . ."

"No jokes," she said. "Not today."

"I'm just sayin'."

"Do you think I've *already* gone all the way blind, Brady? Do you think I can't see what you've been doing lately?" She raised an eyebrow at him now, one of her signature moves. "You think I don't know what you're doing?"

"Okay," Nate said. "I'm the one in the dark now, and not just because of the crypt light you've got going in here."

"The light's been hurting my eyes more and more, and I hate wearing those geek glasses, even when I'm alone," she said. "And don't try to change the subject."

"Not sure what the subject is, Abs."

"You and me," she said. "Me and you. *Us.* And the way you've been pushing me away so it won't be hard for me to leave *you* when I leave *here*—if I do end up at Perkins full time—and don't even think about trying to deny it."

"I can't," he said. "Busted."

"You were doing it and I was letting you do it because I thought you might actually be right," Abby said. "So why'd you have to ruin everything by dropping off *this*?"

She held up the box and shook it at him like she was shaking a fist.

"Because I don't want you to go, whether you do or not," he said. "And I couldn't keep lying about that, because I thought the lying might be hurting you more than the truth."

Now she smiled.

Nate didn't want to say this to Abby, not today. But all of a sudden Nate felt like he was seeing things better than he had in a long time, even if the opposite was true for her.

CHAPTER 26

The house was empty again when Nate got home from school the next day.

When he went into the kitchen for his snack, he discovered homemade chocolate chip cookies on the table, which explained why the house smelled like a bakery. Somehow his mom had found time to bake on a day when he knew she'd been there to open The Clairmont Shop at nine in the morning and would be going straight from there to her hostessing job, which meant she wouldn't get home until ten tonight, if she was lucky.

"Maybe the best chocolate chip cookies in all of world history!" was the way the note on the table read.

The note didn't say that the cookies were his mom's way of saying things were still normal in the house, even though they both knew differently.

His dad, Nate knew, had a couple of houses to show to prospective buyers and a job interview after that.

So the house that Nate figured they were on the verge of losing, the house he'd grown up in, the only *home* he'd ever known, was Nate's private property. Again. He wasn't going to be alone that long because Malcolm's mom was picking him up around six, taking him and Malcolm and Pete to Joe's for pizza before they all went to a movie.

His weekend homework could wait until Sunday.

Nate ate some cookies, washed them down with a glass of milk, went upstairs to grab the ball, and went outside to do what he did every single day now, whether he had practice or not:

Take dead aim at the SportStuff target. Try to turn himself back into what his mom still called him, even now.

The boy with the golden arm.

The Valley Patriots had two regular-season games left before he went to Foxboro on Thanksgiving night, and needed to win them both to finish second in the league and qualify for a spot in the championship game, on the second Saturday *after* he made his throw in Foxboro. Nate didn't know if he was going to get the chance to use his arm in those games, had accepted the fact that he might end up doing more to help his team win the title by catching the ball rather than throwing it.

Nate knew he had no control over that, and Coach always said to worry only about the things in sports that you could control.

Out here in the backyard, though, alone with his ball and the target, Nate was in control. He was a quarterback again, trying to get his head and his arm right—maybe even his heart right—to make his Brady throw at Gillette.

And the only way to get himself right again, he'd decided,

was to stop complaining about the pressure of it all, even to himself. He wasn't going to talk about pressure or whine about it. Or run from it. He was going to accept it, same as he had being a wide receiver for the rest of the season if that's the way things were going to roll out. He was going to remember the way he used to throw and the player he used to be, the guy who *wanted* the ball in his hands when it was all on the line.

Nate didn't care about being the boy with the golden arm again. He just wanted to be that guy.

His mom didn't complain about having to hold down two jobs, and lately his dad was back to being his old dad, even without his old job, out there every day trying to sell houses, trying to get just one sale on somebody else's house so they didn't lose theirs.

Abby's world was shrinking one day at a time and yet she *never* complained.

Nate thought about her now, between throws, heard her telling him that on the bus ride home today:

"I can't say 'why me,' Brady. That's one of the big no-can-do's. Because if I do that now that bad stuff has happened to me, why didn't I say it about all the amazing stuff that happened to me before? Including having a total goofball as my best friend on the entire planet."

It was right then that Nate had decided to ask himself a different question, from now until Thanksgiving night:

Not, Why me?

Instead: *Why not?*

Why not make the throw?

Why not win the money and feel like he'd won more than all of Tom Brady's Super Bowls combined?

So he was out here today and every day, the kid they all called "Brady," pretending that he really was. Some days he'd make the first throw he tried. Sometimes it would take him half an hour. Or more. Sometimes he wouldn't be able to get out here until after practice and after dinner and he'd be trying to put the ball through that twenty-inch hole using only the porch lights and, on really clear nights, the light of the moon.

Sometimes he brought out a bag of balls, firing them one after another at the target. Sometimes he brought out just the one, the way he had today, telling himself this was his money ball, but making himself chase it every time he missed.

Today he told himself he wasn't going back inside until he made a total of five, even if he was still out here when Malcolm's mom pulled into the driveway.

He kept saying to his mom that maybe he should try to find himself an after-school job.

Now he had.

CHAPTER 27

Nate," Coach Rivers said. "Go in for Eric."

They were a minute into the fourth quarter, Valley ahead of Westboro 14–7. And suddenly Nate was the Patriots' quarterback again.

Eric had hit his passing hand on a Westboro helmet early in the third quarter, actually completing a pass to Nate that became his first touchdown as a wide receiver. The cornerback covering him had tried to take an amazingly dumb chance going for the interception—dumb because it was just him and Nate alone on the sideline—and totally missed the ball. Nate didn't.

He looked the sucker right into his hands, turned around, and saw all this green grass ahead of him, like a stretch of open road. Thirty yards later he had his first touchdown.

It was after LaDell had run it in for the conversion that Nate noticed Eric holding his right hand in his left, telling Coach it still stung a little but just needed some ice. Nate would have said the same thing, knowing that Eric didn't want to come out, not just because of the way he was playing, but because *he* was the Patriots' quarterback now.

Except Eric hadn't completed a pass since he'd gotten the stinger on his throwing hand. And even though Valley's defense hadn't let Westboro's Falcons cross midfield in the second half, it was still just a one-touchdown game. So when Eric got sacked on first down all the way back on the Valley 15-yard line and came up shaking his right hand again, Coach Rivers gave Nate the call.

Nate, who'd just come out of the game for a one-play breather, tipped his helmet back now for a fast swig of Gatorade. Then he pulled down so hard on his face mask he was afraid it might come off in his hand.

"You ready?" Coach said.

"You know something, Coach?" Nate said. "I am."

Coach Hanratty told him the play. Nate sprinted toward the huddle. Right before he knelt down to tell the guys what they were going to run, he gave a look into the stands, to where his parents were sitting, Abby between them.

He didn't think she could see him. But she was here, that was what mattered. She was in the stands, and he was about to be under center again.

The way things used to be.

Malcolm spoke before he did.

"Welcome back," he said to Nate.

The Patriots ran a neat draw on first down, Malcolm knocking over their nose tackle as easily as if the kid were an inflatable toy, enabling LaDell to run for twenty yards. Just like that, they were out to their own 35. Then they ran Ben on a sweep around Bradley's end and got ten more. Nate was fine with them running the ball this way, didn't care how they racked up first downs. He just loved being the guy calling the signals again, loved standing behind Malcolm, loved the feeling of them moving the ball.

Loved being back, even if he hadn't really *gone* anywhere.

If they didn't throw the rest of the game, he was down with that as long as they won, won their chance to beat Dennison the next week and get into the title game.

First-and-ten from the 45.

Nate looked over to Coach Hanratty for his hot read.

It was "P-Square."

Nate smiled. This wasn't some kind of math problem Coach Hanratty was sending in. Wasn't even a square-out route for Pete. It was just the official new playbook name for the Hutchins-and-Go.

Pete would line up tight to the line of scrimmage, would make a square-out move to the outside, even look back at Nate and wave for the ball as he did. When he did, Nate was supposed to deliver a pump fake that was good enough to win an Academy Award, and then Pete Mullaney was supposed to run down the sideline as if bad dogs were chasing him and wait for Nate to deliver the goods.

And if he still *could* deliver, they were going to be two touchdowns ahead of Westboro.

Not just a good kind of pressure now, he told himself.

The *best*.

Nate took the handoff from Malcolm, faked one to LaDell, stood tall in the pocket again, watched the play begin to develop, seeing it all in slow motion, the way he used to in moments like this. Saw Pete making his sharp cut. Saw Pete's hand shoot into the air. Then Nate brought the ball forward, squeezing it as he did, making sure not to sell the fake so well that the ball squirted out of his hand.

The cornerback bought it like popcorn at the movies.

As soon as he did, Pete was gone.

For the first time in a long time, in a place other than his backyard, Nate didn't worry about how much air to put under the ball or how hard to throw it. Didn't worry about missing or getting intercepted. Didn't worry period.

All he knew was this: ball and target.

Nate didn't hesitate, just threw what turned out to be a spiral tighter than old sneakers.

He watched the ball only briefly. Because he knew. Sometimes you just did. He stepped outside the pocket now, out from behind Malcolm, put his right fist in the air and began pumping it hard, like he was trying to punch a hole in the top of the sky.

Money ball.

When he looked down the field again, Pete was crossing the goal line with the touchdown that made it 20–7, Valley. The home crowd erupted behind him. Nate turned and saw Abby high-fiving his mom, because in this moment she didn't have to see anything.

All she had to do was listen.

It was the only throw Nate needed to complete the rest of the game, even though he completed a couple of key third-down passes to keep control of the ball and the clock. Final score: Valley 21, Westboro 14.

They were now one win away now from playing for the league championship. But Nate already felt as though he'd won some kind of championship today. Maybe of himself. When it was over, Coach Rivers presented him with the game ball in front of the team. Nate put it under his arm, imagining himself running all the way home with it. Instead he walked over to where his parents were waiting for him at the bottom of the bleachers with Abby.

Nate knew she'd brought her cane with her, but he didn't see it in her hand now, which meant she'd persuaded Nate's mom to let her leave it in the car.

After his parents hugged him, Abby said, "You were great today, Brady."

"Probably because you were here to see it," Nate said, not even worried about saying it that way, not knowing how much she really *had* seen.

"Nothing I hadn't seen before," she said. "It was like a movie I'd watched over and over again."

They started walking toward the parking lot, Nate's parents leading the way. Nate reached over with his free hand and gently took Abby's arm. She let him.

In a quiet voice he said, "Did you really see, Abs?"

"Everything," she said.

He wanted to believe her. And so he did.

CHAPTER 28

Nate felt good about football again. At least he had that going for him.

He wasn't kidding himself, wasn't living in some kind of dream world. He didn't think that everything had turned around because he had completed a few passes in an eighth-grade football game. He knew he still had work to do.

But at least his arm seemed to be working again. Not just in the game, but also when he returned to practice Tuesday night. Eric was still the starter, that hadn't changed. But when Nate got his snaps, he moved the team again, and did so with sharp, accurate passes. It made him feel as if his head were screwed on right again, at least when a helmet was attached to it.

The doorbell rang after school on Wednesday. Nate was alone in the house and thought it might be some kind of delivery. It wasn't.

It was Abby.

This time she had her cane with her. She smiled at him when he opened the front door, but the smile had nothing behind it.

"Care to donate to the blind?" she said.

Weak joke, told in a weak voice.

"Hey," he said.

"That wasn't funny, was it?" Abby said.

"Well, let's just say it wasn't up to your usual standards."

Nate stepped out on the porch, looked around. "How'd you get here?"

"I was out walking," she said, "and I finally realized I was walking straight over here."

"By yourself?"

She held up the cane, waved it at him like it was a sword. "I go out and practice with this thing sometimes," she said. "It's why I'm getting pretty handy with it. I don't use it every step of the way, but it helps me out with stuff . . . I don't see so well anymore. Like curbs."

"You have trouble even seeing *curbs*?"

Abby said, "Know how you're on the beach on a gray day like this and you can't tell where the water ends and the sky begins? It's getting like that when I'm out walking. So I bring my trusty cane and I don't stumble as much."

"Does your mom know you came all the way here?"

"She probably doesn't even know I went out. She and my dad . . ."

And just like that the girl who never cried, at least in front of Nate, started to cry now.

"Abs," he said. "What happened?"

"My dad lost his job," she said.

"*Your* dad? Lost *his* job. At the *bank*?"

She looked at him and nodded.

"He actually lost it two weeks ago, just without telling me," she said.

"That's terrible, Abs," Nate said. "Listen, I know it would be terrible news for anybody. I know it was for us." Trying to find anything that would make her stop crying. "But you guys aren't us," he said. "I mean, you guys have a lot of money."

Abby said, "Not anymore."

Her dad's bank had been bought by a much bigger bank. Nate remembered Abby talking about that right after school started, but Nate hadn't paid much attention. He just assumed that people like his dad could lose their jobs, but not somebody like Abby's, who was always flying off to do business all over the country.

Only now the new bank had let him go, nice knowing you, good-bye.

"Can't he just find a job with another bank?" Nate said. "Come on, Abs, my family worries about money, not yours."

"He says there was a time when it would have been easy, hauling off and getting a job just as good as the one he had," she said. "But things have changed, Brady. My dad says that the way things are going with the economy, pretty soon there are going to be about five or six big banks left and that's going to be it."

Nate wondered if there really was going to be a time, ever

again, when *economy* didn't make you think of a hurricane that kept blowing through people's lives. You were going along, having what felt like a pretty cool life, and then all of a sudden came the *economy* trying to wreck everything.

"He tried to explain it to me until I just stopped hearing what he was saying," Abby said. "But I get the picture. We had a lot of our money in stocks and now most of it is just . . . gone. Along with our health insurance."

Nate realized now, like a dope, that they were still standing at the front door. He motioned for Abby to follow him in and closed the door behind them. The two of them went into the family room, Nate's game-watching room. He asked if she wanted something to drink. She said no. He asked if she was hungry. She said no, telling him to stop trying to be the perfect host.

"I'm just saying," he said. "Anything you want, you tell me."

"I want to be with you," she said.

"It'll be all right," he said.

She closed her eyes, squeezing them shut, a couple more tears managing to escape.

"I keep telling myself that," she said. "I really do. And most times I can make myself believe it." Even now, he thought, she wouldn't give in to feeling sorry for herself, even now, when Nate wanted to throw a penalty flag at the whole world for piling on the person who least deserved it. "Just not today," she said. "It's just like . . ."

For once he could read her mind.

"One more thing," he said.

"Yeah," she said. "One more thing. And I can't handle one more thing, Brady."

He wanted to tell her so many things, wanted to tell her that she couldn't worry about money, shouldn't worry about money, that there were much more important things to worry about than that, that he'd finally figured out that worrying didn't help anything or solve anything.

Mostly he wanted her to stop crying.

So he did something he'd never done before then: He put his arm around Abby McCall and pulled her close to him. She let him, resting her head on his shoulder. And the two of them just sat there, not moving, for what felt like a very long time, until he finally said, "It *is* going to be all right, Abs."

She stayed where she was, pressed into his shoulder, and asked how he knew that.

Nate said he just did, that she was going to have to take that one on faith, told the girl going blind something his mom told him all the time, that sometimes faith was believing in things *nobody* could see.

CHAPTER 29

Big-game Saturday, on the road, against the Dennison Browns.

Twelve days before Thanksgiving.

The Patriots were tied with the Browns for second place in the league. So the last game of the regular season was really like the first game of the playoffs. Win and you got to keep playing, got the chance to play undefeated Blair and old pal Willie Clifton, in the championship game in two weeks.

Lose and go home.

Lose and the next game they all got to play would be in freshman football next year, or varsity, if any of them were good enough to make the varsity as freshmen.

But that was next season. Blair was the week after next, if they could make it that far. All that mattered—in football, anyway—was this game, today. This Saturday afternoon.

Some week, Nate thought. Last Saturday he had become a quarterback again, even if he was still a backup, even if it had been only for a quarter. Wednesday he had found out about Abby's dad.

Yesterday, on the bus home from school, Abby had told him she would be going back to Boston next week to spend a few days at the hospital, go through some new tests, see if there was anything they could do—in Abby's words—to slow down the whole stupid process of Leber's, a dirtier word to Nate than *economy*.

"Like an operation?" Nate had said.

"No, no, no," Abby had said. "Just more tests, don't worry. But when they're done, they'll probably decide whether it really is time for me to check into old Perkins for good."

Nate had said, "Man, is there anything else that's going to happen this week?"

"Yeah," Abby had said, giving him the raised eyebrow. "We're going to beat the living daylights out of Dennison."

He was going to try his hardest to get that one done, try not to think about everything that was happening around him, everything that was *about* to happen.

For this one day, he would try to concentrate only on football, be the guy who'd always been at his best no matter how crazy the game got around him. He would feel like the game really was in his hands.

Except it wasn't anymore. Even on a great football day like this, the stands full on both sides of the field, the game was still going to be in Nate's hands only when Eric put it there.

Coach Rivers' pregame speech today was the shortest Nate could ever remember. He gathered them all in front of the visitors'

bench maybe a minute before the opening kickoff and said, "Anybody here ready for it to be basketball season?"

"*No!*" the Patriots yelled back at him.

"Didn't think so," Coach said. "I don't even like basketball all that much, to tell you the truth."

Coach liked the way the Patriots started the game even less. They had driven the ball down the field after the opening kickoff, made first down after first down, wound up first-and-goal at the Browns' 2-yard line. But then LaDell, who hardly ever fumbled, got crossed up on a handoff with Eric, left the ball on the ground, and the Browns' nose tackle fell on it.

At least the Browns couldn't move the ball out of there and ended up having to punt out of their own end zone. It wasn't a good punt, so the Patriots started their next drive at the Browns' 20-yard line. On first down Eric tried to hit Nate on an out pass and didn't put nearly enough on the ball. Nate didn't even have enough time to turn himself into a defender and try to knock the ball away from the cornerback covering him. The kid was in full stride when he intercepted the ball. By the time Nate *did* manage to catch him from behind, feeling as if he were chasing the world's fastest human, the cornerback had run all the way to the Patriots' 20-yard line.

Three plays later, Dennison was ahead 7–0.

When the guys on defense came off the field, Malcolm took off his helmet, spit to the side and said, "Two turnovers in the first quarter. It's like we're all doing our community service hours for school right *here.*"

The Patriots made it three turnovers right before the half. They had moved the ball for the first time since their opening drive, throwing every down, Nate having turned into Eric's favorite receiver, catching three passes, all for first downs, making the cornerback who'd made the interception more and more frustrated.

Then Coach Hanratty went to Nate once too often. The middle linebacker read Eric's eyes the whole way on what was supposed to be a little curl pass, Nate running hard for ten yards, turning and looking for the ball. This time it was a big, fast linebacker who seemed to have a full head of steam as the ball ended up in his hands.

Nate started to chase, but ended up on the ground when the cornerback who'd been covering him cut him down with a perfectly legal block from his blind side. Nate watched from the ground as Malcolm missed the tackle, then Sam, and saw the kid with the ball make it to the sideline. Ben Cion had the last clear shot at him, but the linebacker was too strong, just shrugged Ben off and kept going, all the way to the end zone. After the conversion it was 14–0 for the Browns.

That's the way the half ended, and the way the season was going to end if they didn't change something, and fast.

So Coach Rivers changed quarterbacks.

He didn't make the announcement in front of the team, just to Nate and Eric, pulling both of them aside.

"We're gonna play this out the way we came in," he said. "With Nate under center."

Right away Eric said, "I'm good with that, Coach." Then he turned to Nate, grinning, and said, "I'm a better receiver than you anyway."

"True dat," Nate said.

Coach Rivers told Nate to go get loose. The Patriots would be receiving the second-half kickoff and they were going to come out firing. Nate went and grabbed a ball and Eric went with him, the two of them behind the bench, Nate warming up fast, throwing the ball as soon as he caught it, like he was a pitcher warming up in the bullpen, runners all over the bases.

It was after he heard the ref's whistle that he heard Abby's voice.

"Hey, you," she said. "Hey, Brady."

She was wearing a Patriots cap on her head, a gray Patriots hoodie.

"What are you doing down here?" Nate said.

"Getting a better view, silly."

"Still trying to get into my head," he said.

"I was never out of it," Abby said. "Now go win the game."

He started doing just that on the second series of the second half, after the two teams had traded punts. The Patriots had the ball on their own 49, and Nate went to work. They had been trying to mix passes and running plays for most of the game, but now Coach Hanratty called for five straight passes, to five different receivers.

Ben caught the first, then Bradley, then Pete and Eric and

LaDell. The one to LaDell was a perfect screen, against a blitz, and he ran it all the way to the Browns' 3-yard line. Nate took it in from there, rolling to his right, arm up like he was passing the whole time, freezing the linebackers, never planning to do anything except run it in. Nobody laid a hand on him, and after Ben ran off tackle for the conversion, it was 14–7.

The Patriots were back in the game. And Nate was feeling it.

On the third Valley possession of the fourth quarter, with five minutes left in the game, Nate dropped back in the pocket and threw a perfect spiral to a wide-open Pete running a straight fly route. Another Valley touchdown. LaDell ran the conversion in this time.

Game tied, 14–all. And the Patriots had every ounce of momentum on their side.

One more score and they would go to the championship game. Or, just as possible, one Dennison score and *they* would go. Now what felt like the first game of the playoffs had turned into sudden death.

Before they kicked the ball off, Malcolm Burnley came over to Nate.

"I like basketball, don't get me wrong," he said.

Nate grinned. "Nothing better than that first day back in the gym."

"But I believe," Malcolm said, "that I would like to have me one more big football game before we go there."

Then he banged his helmet, hard, against Nate's the way the

linemen did with each other all the time and said, "We're gonna go out and stop these suckers now. Then you're gonna get back on the field and take us on home."

"I'm supposed to do all that for *free*?" Nate said.

"Well, I can't pay you a million dollars," Malcolm said. "But I will take you to Joe's afterward."

"Who could pass up a sweet offer like that?" Nate said.

Malcolm made sure Nate had his chance. On third-and-two for the Browns, Malcolm steamrolled his way into the backfield and sacked the quarterback. The Browns were forced to punt. Ben made a fair catch at the Patriots' 40-yard line. With two minutes and change left, the game was still tied.

In the huddle Nate said, "Okay, this is the way we roll," and told them the play. "Exit 15 E," they called it. A fifteen-yard square-out to Eric, a timing route. Done right, the ball would be waiting for Eric as he turned back to face Nate. Nate just managed to get the pass off before he got flattened by the Browns' blitzing middle linebacker. He only found out when he got up that he'd thrown a strike to Eric.

First down Patriots, on the Browns' 48.

Nate nearly got buried again on the very next play, barely managed to throw the ball away before what felt like the entire Browns' front four hit him.

When he went down, somebody stepped on his right hand.

He didn't know who got him. Could have been one of his own blockers. All Nate did know was how much it hurt. Like someone had jabbed a needle right into the top of his hand.

He didn't cry out at the bottom of the pile. Didn't grab the hand when he stood up, as much as he wanted to, not wanting anybody to know he was in any kind of pain. Just waited for the pain to go away.

Only it didn't.

When he got back in the huddle, leaning forward, hands on knees, he was at least able to make a fist, figuring that if he could do that, he hadn't done anything really bad. Like break something.

Nate wished he could call a time-out, put some ice on it, even if it was just for a minute. But they weren't wasting one of the two time-outs they had left. And then everybody would see he'd done something to his throwing hand, including his coaches. Who might want to take him out.

And Nate had decided: He wasn't coming out until next season.

He got the read off Coach Hanratty's board. Another pass, this one to Bradley. It made Nate smile, made him think of one of his mom's expressions: no rest for the weary. He was going to keep throwing, sore hand or not, until they were in the end zone.

"You okay?" Malcolm said when they broke the huddle.

"Yeah. Just got the wind knocked out of me," Nate said.

He got under center and made sure to receive Malcolm's snap with his bottom hand, his left hand, more than his right. He felt a quick jolt of pain anyway. But then his hand was on the laces and he was dropping back into the pocket, and the only thing that concerned him was delivering the ball to Bradley over the middle with something on it.

He did. A perfect spiral. Bradley gathered it in and fell forward to the Browns' 36-yard line.

A minute and thirty left.

They crossed the Browns up then, running the ball twice in a row in their hurry-up offense, the second time on a direct snap to LaDell with Nate lined up in the shotgun. They had another first down and Nate called his second-to-last time-out. Thirty seconds left. Ball on the Browns' 24.

Plenty of time.

As Nate walked toward the huddle, he looked over to the sideline, past his bench. Abby was right where he'd left her, staring right at him. He patted his heart twice and hoped she saw.

Their last run of the day was a quarterback draw by Nate. He ran up the middle, thought he might go all the way, but got tackled from behind at the Browns' 10.

First down and goal.

He spiked the ball, wanting to hold on to that last time-out for dear life.

Eighteen seconds left.

He looked over to Coach Hanratty. The hot read was the same

play they'd run to Bradley a few plays before, only this time Bradley was supposed to be right between the goalposts when he came open.

As though Bradley were the SportStuff target now.

There was this amazing quiet you got in the huddle sometimes, even in moments like this, even when it was all on the line, even with both the Dennison fans and the Valley fans making as much noise as they were. Nate looked up into the faces of his teammates. He smiled and told them the play, feeling the way he hoped they all felt:

That this was exactly where they were all supposed to be.

He set up in the shotgun. Malcolm gave him a perfect snap and even with that, Nate fumbled it briefly, being too careful to protect his right hand. But then he got a handle on it and took a couple of extra steps back.

Watched it all play out in front of him.

Watched as everything seemed to happen at once.

Bradley made his cut, broke free, turned around between the posts. The ball, a bullet, was already halfway there. The force of the pass seemed to surprise even Bradley, as many times as he'd caught Nate's fastball, as much arm as he knew Nate had. This one knocked him backward and knocked him over.

But his feet were still in bounds when he landed, and so was Bradley, and the ball was cradled to his chest.

Valley 20, Dennison 14.

Eight seconds left.

For the conversion Nate threw a fade to Eric in the corner and he outjumped the safety for it. Valley 21, Dennison 14.

Malcolm squibbed the kickoff. It seemed like half the Valley team tackled the kid with the ball, absolutely buried him at the Browns' 35.

The horn sounded. The Valley Patriots were in the championship game against Blair. It was still football season after all.

CHAPTER 30

Abby's doctor had to push back her tests a week because he was called out of town. So Nate didn't have to say good-bye to her until the Sunday before Thanksgiving, four days until the big throw.

Only the throw didn't feel nearly as big right now as Abby leaving, even if he was sure in his heart that it wasn't for good.

Man, Nate thought. Man man *man*.

How did we ever get here?

It seemed like just the other day that she was standing next to him at the SportStuff counter, practically ordering him to sign up for the contest. Now she was going into the hospital and might be going off to Perkins for good after that and there was a "For Sale" sign in front of her house same as there was Nate's. And there was so much he wanted to say to her, so much he felt like he *needed* to say. But he didn't, not wanting to make things worse—at least for now, he kept telling himself—than they already were.

So the two of them stood in her studio, what had always been her special place, all of her paintings still covered, while her parents packed up the car.

"How's the hand, by the way?" Abby said.

"Perfect."

"Liar."

"It must be exhausting," he said, "knowing all the answers before you even ask the questions."

"Well, it is, actually," she said, smiling. Doing anything to lighten the mood. "But then I lie down and take a little rest, and I'm as brilliant as ever."

She was the only one he'd told about getting stepped on, making her promise not to tell anybody else. The hand was still stiff a week later, and he still wasn't able to grip the ball as firmly as he wanted to, which took some of the snap off his throws. But the coaches hadn't said anything or seemed to notice anything wrong, and neither had any of his receivers. Nate wasn't throwing as accurately at the target in the backyard, but he told himself that was just nerves as the big night got closer.

He'd told Abby because, as always, she saw right through him and kept asking him what was wrong. He couldn't lie to her.

Now in her studio she said, "I don't see why you couldn't even tell your parents."

"I explained that," he said. "I don't want there to be any excuses if I miss."

"You're not missing, remember?"

"Right," he said. "Silly me. How could I forget?"

He sat down in his chair. She was standing in the middle of

the room, staring at him. There was more on his mind than a hurt hand.

"What aren't you telling me?" she asked.

"Nothing," he said. "I'm just relaxing. And my hand is fine."

"There's something else," she said.

"Abs, I know you've heard this from me before, but I have no idea what you're talking about."

"You holding back on me, Brady?"

"Just holding back so I don't start blubbering like a little girl."

"Okay," she said. "That is extremely insulting to little girls."

"Good point."

"So you're not holding back?" Still staring at him, as if she still had 20/20, even though she could see only a few feet in front of her now.

If that.

"Holding on is more like it."

"You'll see me on Thursday night, remember?"

"You promise you'll be there?"

Abby patted her heart the way he did on the field. "Promise."

Her mom called up to her then, said it was time for them to go to Boston. Abby closed the space between them at what felt like the speed of light, or sound, and hugged Nate as hard then as she ever had, as if she never wanted to let go.

"Love you, Brady," she said.

"Me too."

"You're gonna make it."

"We're both gonna make it," Nate said.

"I still believe in happy endings," Abby said. "Just so you know."

"Me too," Nate said again.

They walked down the stairs together, Nate taking great care that she didn't see his arm behind her, ready to catch her if she stumbled, even though she was using her cane.

When they were on the front walk, Abby's mom and dad wished Nate luck, told him they were rooting for him, said they'd see him on Thursday night in Foxboro.

Nate shook hands with Mr. McCall and then Mrs. McCall. He didn't say anything more to Abby. They'd said everything they needed to say to each other upstairs.

He watched her climb into the backseat, hook up her seat belt, smile at him through the window, and press her hand to the window. Nate pressed his against the outside. Then he heard Mr. McCall start up the car and slowly back it out of the driveway, away from the big, expensive house that was as much for sale as his was.

Nate walked out to the street and watched the car make a right turn on Eden Road. He stood there watching even when he knew Abby couldn't see him anymore.

Stood there wondering about happy endings, and just how many of those you could hope for in your life.

Then he rode his bike home and got his ball and tried to throw it through a twenty-inch hole, making sure he followed through even when his hand hurt, making three the number today, telling himself he wasn't going inside until he put it through the hole that many times.

He was working on number three when the back door opened and his dad shouted loud enough for the whole neighborhood to hear. He'd made a sale on a house, a big one on the north side of town.

Nate smiled. Then he turned and made one more throw.

Money.

CHAPTER 31

They had decided, unanimously, that they would celebrate Thanksgiving on Friday, that there would be no turkey or Thanksgiving dinner or anything else until they got back from Foxboro. No matter what happened in Foxboro.

The SportStuff people had arranged for them to spend Wednesday night at a Courtyard Boston hotel, just a few minutes away from Gillette Stadium. A limousine would pick them up at five o'clock, even though kickoff wasn't until eight thirty. Nate and his dad knew why. They'd seen firsthand when they came to Patriots games that traffic getting in and out of Gillette could be rougher than the Patriots' defense.

As soon as they arrived at VIP parking, they were to be greeted by Doug Compton, SportStuff's vice president in charge of public relations, who would take them up to the company's luxury suite.

He'd told them the day before they could "relax" up there.

"Yeah," Nate said in the back of the limousine, the first limousine ride of his life. "That's what I'm planning to do between now and halftime. Relax. You guys'll probably have to wake me up from my nap so I don't sleep through the throw."

"You look calm enough to me," his mom said.

"Cool as a cucumber," his dad said.

Nate shook his head. "Whatever veggie's *not* cool? That's me."

Malcolm was sitting next to him, having made the trip with the Brodies from Valley to Foxboro the night before. Nate had told Malcolm that he wanted him along so he'd have somebody to warm up with, even though Malcolm didn't exactly have the softest hands on the Patriots. That was the cover story, anyway. The real reason was that Malcolm was his best friend on the team and he'd always been able to make Nate feel better about almost everything just by being around.

For tonight, Malcolm was describing himself as Nate's "quality control coach."

"You're gonna be cool because you *are* cool," Malcolm said in the limo. "Gonna be the same on this field as it's gonna be against Blair in the championship game. Nobody is gonna see my man sweat."

"I wish," Nate said.

Doug Compton was waiting for them in VIP parking, as promised. They'd met Doug at the hotel last night, when he'd come over to "walk them through" the halftime show.

"We're rooting for you tonight," Doug said.

Nate said, "But I could cost you a million dollars."

"Nate, listen to me," Doug said. "If a thirteen-year-old boy makes that throw on national television, nobody at our place is going to feel like a loser. You've got to trust me on that one."

Now he handed them all the credentials they were supposed

to wear around their necks. When they were inside, Nate asked Doug Compton to double-check again that the tickets had been left for Abby and her parents. Doug said he would when they got upstairs, then said to Nate, "Well, you look nice and relaxed, considering the circumstances."

Nate looked at Malcolm and rolled his eyes. "Yeah," he said. "Cool as a cucumber."

When they got to the suite, neither Nate nor Malcolm could believe their eyes. "My whole *house* isn't as nice as this," Malcolm said. There was a living area with a huge flat-screen TV that was showing the Cowboys game from Dallas, and a kitchen and four rows of seats looking out at the 45-yard-line, and even a stack of video games and controllers that Doug said SportStuff had ordered for the occasion.

"I don't just want to watch the game from here," Malcolm said. "I want to *move* here."

Doug Compton told everybody to help themselves to food and drinks, that a waiter would be arriving any second, then reminded Nate and his parents that he would walk them downstairs with about five minutes remaining in the first half. When the half ended, he'd take them out on the field along with the president of SportStuff, then Nate would be interviewed briefly by Gil Santos, the Patriots radio play-by-play man, over the stadium's public address system.

"At that point," Doug Compton said, "somebody will hand you the ball."

Nate said, "I brought my own," and opened up the small gym bag he'd brought with him and showed Doug Compton the Brady ball.

Before Doug left, Nate asked if it would be all right for him and Malcolm to go back down to the field for a few minutes, just so he could loosen up a little and get used to the lights, maybe even the wind. He didn't want halftime to be the first time he was on that field. Doug made a quick call on his cell phone, said, "No problem," and then he and Nate and Malcolm went back down the elevator.

Nate wasn't sure what he would feel like in a few hours, when he was making the walk toward the field for real. But even now, walking past the Pats' locker room, his heart was pounding so hard and so fast, making him feel so out of breath, that it was as if he'd skipped the limo ride and *run* all the way here from the hotel.

A lot of the Patriots' players were already on the field. They weren't dressed in full pads yet, no helmets—just sweatshirts, some playing catch, some stretching, some doing wind sprints. All were getting ready for their own big night on Thanksgiving. Nate looked around for Tom Brady, hoping he might be out early, but didn't see him anywhere.

Nate asked Doug Compton again if Abby and her parents

would have the same credentials he had so they'd be able to come down to the field at halftime, too.

If this did end the way Nate wanted it to, she had to be there.

"Just spoke to them," Doug said. "On her mom's cell. They hit some traffic but got to the suite right after we came down here. So no worries. Why don't you go get your throwing in? SportStuff has a lot of juice around here, but they're not going to let us stay on the field forever."

Nate and Malcolm went over and began soft-tossing behind the Patriots' bench. Nate took his time between throws so he could look around, at the open end of the stadium, at the Sport-Stuff signs and an even bigger one for F. W. Webb, the huge Gillette sign over the scoreboard. Finally seeing the world of pro football—Brady's world—from the inside. The lights. The signs. The fans starting to fill the seats. The wire over his head, the one with the camera attached to it, zooming along this way and that, as if the camera were warming up, too, for when it would give people watching on television those amazing overhead shots.

Nate even noticed how green the grass was, how white the white of the hash marks looked from down here, how bright the colors of the lettering for "Patriots" in the end zones and the Patriots logo on the field.

As bright as Abby colors.

The first time Nate's dad had taken him to Fenway Park, Nate had been surprised that the place looked even smaller than he'd expected from watching on television. Gillette Stadium was bigger. He thought, Everything is bigger tonight.

Except maybe the target.

All along, every day of practice, every night when this throw was the last thing he'd think about—when he wasn't thinking about what was happening with Abby—Nate kept telling himself the same thing: It would be the same target in Gillette that he was throwing to in his backyard. Only now, standing on this field, he knew better. Now even the thought of the pep talks he'd been giving himself made him laugh out loud, loud enough for Malcolm to hear over the pregame rock music being piped into Gillette Stadium.

Malcolm yelled down to him, "What's so funny?"

Nate put the Brady ball under his arm and made a gesture with his left hand that tried to take in the whole stadium.

"This!" he yelled back. "Us being here. Me trying to make the throw tonight."

"And this . . . amuses you?"

"Yeah, it kind of does," Nate said.

Nate threw him one last pass, a spiral so tight the ball seemed to shrink in the air, then signaled that he was finished. Malcolm jogged over to him and handed him back the ball.

"You always tell me that winning's more fun than anything," Malcolm said. "Well, tonight you're gonna win something people will never forget, and turn this into the funnest night of your life."

Nate knelt down behind the bench then, grabbed a clump of grass, a big one, stuck it in the pocket of his jeans. Malcolm gave him a look. Nate said, "Souvenir." Malcolm nodded and grabbed some grass of his own.

Doug Compton led them back toward the tunnel. Malcolm started talking about all the things he'd buy for himself with a million dollars if he only had to spend it on himself: flat screens, an iPhone, every cool video game known to man, season tickets to the Patriots' games, and a fancy sports car that he would hold on to until he was old enough to drive it to Gillette Stadium.

"What about you?" he said to Nate. "You must've thought about it."

"Yeah, dude," Nate said. "I have."

"So, you gonna tell?"

Nate smiled and shook his head. "It's like you don't tell what your wish is before you blow out the candles," he said.

Nate believed it.

He believed, tonight more than ever, that if you said it out loud, about the million bucks, it would never happen in a million years.

For most of the first half, what turned out to be a dream first half for Brady and the Patriots, Nate focused on every move the quarterback made. Thinking he might never have a view of a quarterback this good again. And knowing he'd better appreciate it, knowing how quickly things could change, how quickly things had changed for Tom Brady the day he'd gotten hurt.

It had been harder for him to come back than anybody had ever expected. There had been complicatons after the first surgery followed by more setbacks and then even more surgery, which meant starting rehab all over again. Some people wondered if he would ever play again. But finally, Tom Brady was back. Boy, was he ever back—and playing as if he'd never been away, completing the first fourteen passes he attempted, three of them for touchdowns. He was in complete command of himself and his team, and if you watched him move around in the pocket, you wouldn't have known that anything had ever happened to one of his knees. The Patriots didn't even attempt a punt until their second possession of the second quarter.

"Your guy isn't cheating us tonight, is he?" Nate's dad said, sitting next to him in the front row of the suite.

Nate said, "You think he'd mind making my throw for me? Because he hasn't missed anything he's aimed at all night."

Abby punched Nate from the row behind him. "You're not missing either, Brodie."

"I'm *Brodie* now?" he said.

Nate turned around, saw Abby squinting at the field, where Brady had just completed another pass down the field to Randy Moss. "He's Brady tonight," she said. "You're Brodie."

Nate had been trying not to look at the clock too much, not even sure if he wanted it to go slower or faster. But before long there was five twenty eight showing on the game clock. He heard a knock on the window from inside and saw Doug Compton and the president of SportStuff, Mr. Levine, waving at him. Nate's mom was with them. Then Doug smiled and pointed at his watch.

Nate walked back inside and his mom said, "Showtime."

Mr. and Mrs. McCall said they were too nervous, they were going to stay upstairs, watch from here. So the rest of them formed a caravan as they walked down the hall to the elevator bank: Nate, his parents, Abby, Malcolm, Doug Compton, Mr. Levine.

It was then that Doug noticed that Nate was bringing his ball with him.

"Whose autograph?" Doug said, pointing at the ball.

"Tom Brady," Nate said.

"Should've known," Doug said. Then he smiled and said, "Absolutely perfect."

By the time they were at the entrance to the tunnel, watching the game from there, Brady had thrown his fourth touchdown pass of the half and the Patriots were ahead 28–7. Major beatdown. It wasn't ever going to make up for that loss to the Giants in the Super Bowl a few years before, the night in Arizona when the Patriots were trying to go undefeated for a whole season, but for tonight it would do.

I'm the one trying to go undefeated tonight, Nate thought, not Brady.

When the half ended, the players from both teams went running right past them, all of them seeming to arrive at once. Nate tried to spot Brady but couldn't, figuring he must be hidden by a bunch of linemen who up close looked as big as SUVs.

"Okay," Nate's dad said, "let's do this," and then Doug Compton led them all toward the other end of the field, where Nate could see workmen wheeling out the SportStuff target.

Abby was holding on to Nate. No cane tonight. No special glasses, even with the stadium lights as bright as they were. She gave his arm a squeeze.

"You ready?"

"No," he said.

She laughed, hooked her arm inside his now, totally the old Abby in that moment. "C'mon," she said. "It's going to be great."

Malcolm walked on the other side of him. Nate's mom and dad were behind him. Nate forced himself to stop looking around now, to stop looking into the stands and at the television cameraman walking along with them, his camera trained on Nate, all the other cameramen taking their place up near the 30-yard line.

Nate tried to keep his eyes on the target.

Now he heard Gil Santos, the voice of the Patriots for a period that Nate's dad described as forever, welcoming everybody to a very special Thanksgiving halftime show, explaining to the people in the stands that thirteen-year-old Nate Brodie of Valley, Massachusetts, was about to try to throw a football through the hole in the middle of the SportStuff target to win a million dollars for himself and his family.

"Here they are crossing midfield right now!" Gil Santos said. "So let's give a rousing Gillette Stadium welcome to the young man of the hour . . . *Nate Brodie!*"

Then they were all walking into the most incredible sound Nate had ever heard, one he couldn't believe was for him. The force of it seemed to knock the air out of him, making him feel at the same time as if his legs had stopped working.

"Wow!" Abby yelled. "Wow wow wow!"

"Yeah," Malcolm said. "What she said."

Somehow Nate kept walking.

They stopped at the 40, ten yards from where Nate would make the throw. Somehow it seemed more cameramen and photographers had appeared, out of nowhere. Gil Santos introduced Mr. Levine, who waved to the crowd.

Then Gil Santos motioned for Nate to come forward.

"Are you possibly ready for this, Nate?" Gil said when Nate was standing next to him.

Nate swallowed and said, "I better be."

The crowd cheered.

"Then we are just about ready to get this party started," Gil Santos said. "But before we do, you probably want to warm up, right?"

"Yes, sir," Nate said, and was about to tell him that's why he'd brought his friend Malcolm with him, give Malcolm a shout-out to the crowd.

But before he could, Gil Santos said, "Well, if you're going to warm up, you probably want to do that with your quarterback coach, don't you, Nate?"

"My coach . . . ?" Nate said.

Then Gil was shouting into his microphone and over the Gillette Stadium sound system, "Tom Brady, why don't you come over here and give Nate some last-minute advice!"

There was another cheer then, louder than before, louder than anything, as the Patriots' No. 12 came running out of the tunnel.

CHAPTER 32

He was bigger than Nate had thought, just like the stadium had been.

He didn't have his helmet with him, and his hair was all over the place, looking as it usually did, as if the best quarterback in the world had cut his hair himself.

"Nice to meet you, Nate," he said, putting out his right hand.

And Nate was so flustered, so excited to be actually shaking Brady's hand—with his hands shaking the way they were—that he forgot he was holding his football and promptly dropped it.

Brady laughed. Somehow so did Nate, feeling as if he'd used up all the available air in his body. "They told me you're a QB yourself, right?" Brady said. Nate nodded. "Then you know," Tom Brady said. "*Never* put the ball on the ground."

Before Nate could reach down to pick the ball up, Brady beat him to it. As he did, he looked at the signature and smiled.

"This yours?" he said to Nate.

"Bought it with my own money."

"And you're using this one to make the throw?"

"Yeah," Nate said.

"Wow, now the pressure's on me, too," Brady said. "I've *got* to come through for you."

Then Nate said what he'd said upstairs, told Tom Brady he was welcome to make the throw for him, and Brady said, "Nah, Nate. Right now you're the man out here. Now let me see the arm."

Like it was the two of them out at Coppo. Brady was the one who ran up the field, turned around, motioned for Nate to throw him the ball. Nate did. It wobbled a little, but got there. Him and Tom Brady, having a game of catch at Gillette. The crowd roared. Brady threw the ball back, making it look as easy as he had in the first half. The crowd roared again.

Somehow, even knowing what was about to happen, Nate didn't want this part of the night to end.

They threw it back and forth to each other a few more times, Brady acting as if he had all the time in the world. Finally Brady walked back to Nate, put his arm around his shoulders.

"That first Super Bowl," he said, "nobody—and I mean nobody—thought I could take our team down the field. But it didn't matter. Because *I* believed. So *you* believe, okay?"

"Okay," Nate said. "But you couldn't have been as scared in the Superdome as I am right now."

"But, see, that's the beauty of sports," Tom Brady said. "I still get scared. But I never stop believing. The way I never stopped believing I would come back and play this way again after my knee surgeries." Then he said something Nate couldn't believe, as if he'd gotten inside Nate's head. "Now go make this movie come out the way you want it to."

Brady handed the ball back to him, went over and stood with Nate's parents, and Abby, and Malcolm.

Now Gil Santos said, "So this is the moment we've all been waiting for. And *you've* been waiting for, Nate Brodie. Let's see you try to win a million dollars."

In that moment, Nate didn't just hear the noise of Gillette Stadium, he felt it. Then, just as suddenly, it got quiet, at least for him, the way it got quiet at the end of a game.

Nate walked toward the SportStuff logo, the small one they'd made for him at the 30-yard line. His mark. When he got there, he took one last look back, looking at Abby, saw her pat her heart twice.

Believe, the great Tom Brady had said.

And in that moment, Nate did.

He believed as he thought about all the times he'd made this throw behind the house, all the times he'd told himself that he was threading the needle over the middle to Bradley, or Pete, or Eric, or Ben. Ball, target. His dad had told him that from the time the two of them had first gone into the backyard with a football about half the size of the one he held in his right hand now.

The Brady ball, on Brady's field.

With Brady himself a few yards away, watching.

Why not? Nate asked himself, for the very last time.

He didn't wait, didn't hesitate. He had waited long enough. He stepped toward the target, fingers on the laces, like he was stepping up in the pocket.

And released the ball.

High.

That's what he thought, what he was sure of, when he released it.

Only he was wrong.

Maybe because that's not the way the story was supposed to end.

The last few yards the spiral he'd thrown at the SportStuff target looked like an arrow finding a bull's-eye as it sailed cleanly through the hole.

Money.

All the money in the world.

Everything that happened next seemed to happen at once— the explosion of noise that seemed to come crashing down on Nate, the flashing lights all over the stadium, even the fireworks that appeared in the sky.

Nate turned then. And before he looked to Abby, before he looked to his parents, Nate found himself staring right at Tom Brady, smiling at him. Brady smiled back, pumping his fist at him, then pointing as if to say, *You did it.*

So this is what it feels like, Nate wanted to say to him.

This is what it's like to be you.

He'd have to watch the tape later to remember what he'd said into the microphone when it was over. He did remember his mom crying and hugging him. And his dad hugging him and yelling into his ear, "The only kid who could have made that throw just made it."

Then they were bringing out one of those huge fake checks you saw golfers and tennis players get after they won tournaments, the check with "Nate Brodie" on it and "$1,000,000" on the line where the amount was, the check so long that Nate imagined it stretching all the way to the other end zone.

Then Malcolm was on him, lifting him into the air, slapping him one high five after another when he put him down, slapping him so hard it should have made Nate's right hand start hurting again, but Nate was feeling no pain tonight at Gillette Stadium.

"Dude!" Malcolm said. "That was *sick*. Like, one of those *plagues* we read about in history sick."

Nate took a step back, like a fighter covering up, and said, "Dude? Easy on the throwing hand. We've still got one game left to play, remember?"

Malcolm said, "If you can make a throw like that, no *way* we're losing to Blair."

Nate saw Abby then, hanging back, still standing where she'd been before Nate made the throw. She was crying again, he could see, but Nate knew these were happy tears this time. He could see it in those eyes. He walked straight for her, not knowing if the TV cameras were still tracking him or not, not caring. Then he hugged Abby McCall in front of the whole stadium and maybe the whole country. She hugged him back, for all she was worth.

"Did you . . . could you see it go through, Abs?" he said.

She shook her head, and in that moment must have seen the look that started to come across Nate's face like a cloud passing over all the lights of Gillette.

"But don't worry," she said. "It was only because I was watching you the whole time."

"I couldn't have made it without you, Abs," he said.

Now there were no tears, just a huge smile. "Like I don't know that," she said.

They were starting to clear the field now. Nate could hear the public address announcer saying that the second half would be starting shortly.

All of a sudden he and Abby were alone at the 30-yard line, the two of them standing right on top of the SportStuff logo.

"So I've got to ask, Brodie," she said, still calling him that. "What *are* you going to do with all that money?"

Finally, the end of the movie.

"I'm giving it to you," he said. "I found a way for you to see."

CHAPTER 33

You're going to do *what* with all that money?" his mom said.

Friday morning at their house. Thanksgiving with the Brodies, at least as soon as his dad got back. Even on what felt like an instant national sports holiday, his dad was showing two houses this morning, in his new job with Johnson Moriarty, the biggest real estate company in Valley. The job offer had been one of what felt like a hundred messages on their phone when they'd finally gotten home from Foxboro the night before.

Nate thinking it was like one more cool scene, the kind they showed you sometimes when the credits were rolling and you were walking out of the theater.

But for now it was Nate and his mom, bottom of the front stairs.

He decided he'd tell her first, about the surgeon who'd saved the eyesight of a thirteen-year-old boy in London with the same kind of Leber's disease Abby had. The surgeon and the surgery Nate had finally discovered after all those days and nights and searching on the web, sometimes checking every hour on the hour.

He saw the story on Google the same day it showed up on another Web site he'd been going to every day for the last couple of months, run by the Foundation Fighting Blindness.

Not an experimental trial this time, he told his mom, but the real deal, a real-live surgery that had restored the sight of a boy whose vision had started deteriorating at about the same age Abby's had.

His mom knew Nate had been looking into possible surgeries and cures. That's why they'd gone to see Dr. Hunter at Children's Hospital Boston. Yet she didn't know there was a surgery that could give Abby her sight back.

But Dr. Hunter had told him how expensive it was going to be, how much time Abby might have to spend in England.

All that.

Now he told his mom.

"I don't know if it will cost a million, Mom," he said, talking fast. "But it's going to cost a lot, and Abby's dad lost his health insurance and . . . and I don't care, as long as Abby can see again."

She didn't say anything right away, just looked at him, shaking her head. Nate thought she might have some of those happy tears going. "*Always* leading with the heart," she said.

"Something like that," Nate said. "I've been thinking about this for a while."

"Really? I hadn't noticed."

Then his mom said, "You've talked about this with Abby?"

"Not till last night."

"So this was your plan all along. Like one of your game plans."

"You helped by taking me to see Dr. Hunter. He's been in contact with the London doctors ever since." Nate grinned. "And it didn't hurt that I won that little prize by making the throw."

"You're sure about this," his mom said.

"Mom," he said. "I have to do something. It's like a game I can't sit out. Her dad losing his job and the insurance just clinched it. They're barely going to be able to send Abby to Perkins. And besides, we're going to be fine now. I mean moneywise. Aren't we?"

She was smiling again. "We're going to be fine. How could we not be?"

Nate said, "You're the one who's always telling me that the most valuable thing in the world is a random act of kindness, right?"

"Yeah, kiddo. I am."

"Well, now we know how valuable one of those acts can be."

"A million bucks," Sue Brodie said.

"Or as much of it as Abby needs."

His mom was staring again. After all the noise of the night before, the house seemed amazingly quiet right now. Finally she patted her heart twice and reached over so Nate could pound her some fist.

"Well, then," she said. "I guess it's pretty much like your father said last night, right before we walked onto the field."

"What was that?" Nate said.

"Let's do this," she said.

CHAPTER 34

It was just a matter of time now, even with hardly any time left on the clock.

No need for Nate to look over to the sidelines. He already knew what the next play was and, if they didn't score, the play after that.

Nineteen seconds left, first down for Valley from the 42-yard line, down by four points.

That close to the championship. And that far.

He thought of Tom Brady on the field at Gillette, telling him how nobody thought he could do it in that first Super Bowl, when he was the same as a raw rookie.

Maybe people thought that about me this season, Nate thought.

But now he had taken *his* team down the field, and they were this close to pulling it off. Winning the title with a freshman quarterback.

One year and four days since he'd made the million-dollar throw at Gillette. One year exactly since they'd beaten Blair in the eighth-grade championship game.

Time really did fly.

Just not now.

Nate, Malcolm, Pete, LaDell, and the four other freshmen starting for varsity this season would be the youngest Valley team to ever win the league. But only if they could put the ball in the end zone.

Nate did all the talking in the huddle, as usual, even surrounded by so many upperclassmen. Told them the snap count, told Pete not to turn too soon on the Hutchins-and-Go, just to trust it, trust that when he finally turned around, the ball was going to be there.

Nate called the signals from out of the shotgun. He knew Dennison would be coming on the blitz, and they were. But LaDell picked up the outside linebacker. Malcolm seemed to clear out everybody else. Nate had time in the pocket as he watched it all develop, football making as much sense to him as it ever did.

The way his world did now.

As soon as Pete had an inside step on the cornerback, Nate pump-faked the sideline route. The cornerback bit, hard, then was caught flat-footed as Pete spun and sailed down the sideline.

The ball was already on its way.

Pete cradled it in his hands at the fifteen-yard line and sprinted the final steps into the end zone.

The touchdown that gave the Valley Patriots the championship of the Berkshire League. But that wasn't even the best part for Nate, even if he had to admit it was pretty darn good.

The best part was that it wouldn't be Nate's last pass of the day.

Because he'd promised. And you never made a promise, even with your heart, that you couldn't keep.

So after the celebration with his teammates, and after the trophy presentation, after they'd finally cleared the field of players and family and friends, Nate went and collected the game ball from Pete, who hadn't given it up since he'd scored the winning touchdown, and asked if he could borrow it.

Pete handed it over.

Then Nate turned to Abby and said, "Okay, go long."

She was bouncing up and down on her toes, clapping her hands, like the happy kid that she was.

"Got it," she said.

"And remember," Nate said, "*look* the ball all the way into your hands so I don't hit you in the head."

"Not happening," she said. "Not anymore, Brady. Got me the best eyes money can buy now."

She took off down the field then, running on her long legs, long hair flying, *Abby* flying. Nate let the ball go, watched as she ran under it, watched it settle into her hands, watched Abby press it to her chest and keep running, Nate knowing she wasn't stopping until she got to the end zone.

He ran after her then, ran down the open field, knowing nothing could stop either one of them, feeling as if both of them could see forever.

Turn the page for a preview of **Mike Lupica**'s

HERO

THERE were four thugs, total gangsters, in front of the house with their rifles and their night-vision goggles. Four more in back. No telling how many more inside.

So figure a dozen hard guys at least, protecting one of the worst guys in the world.

Not one of them having a clue about how much trouble they were really in, how badly I had them outnumbered.

Hired guns, in any country, never worried me. The Bads? They were the real enemy, worse than any terrorists, even if I was one of the few people alive who knew they existed.

Even my boss, the president of the United States,

didn't know what we were really up against, how much he really needed me.

When he talked about our country fighting an "unseen" threat, he didn't know how true that really was.

When my son, Zach, was little, I used to tell him these fantastic bedtime stories about the Bads, and he thought I was making them up. I wasn't.

The snow was falling hard now, bringing night along with it. Not good. Definitely not good. I didn't need a blizzard tonight, not if I wanted to get the plane in the air once I got back to the small terminal near the airport in Zagreb. Which was only going to happen if I could get past the guards, get inside, and then back out with the guy I'd come all this way for. It meant things going the way they were supposed to, which didn't always happen in my line of work.

My official line of work? That would be special adviser to the president. A title that meant nothing on nights like this. On assignments like this. The real job description was fixing things, things that other people couldn't, saving people who needed saving, capturing people who needed to be stopped. Dispensing my own brand of justice.

Sometimes I had help, people watching my back.

Not tonight. Tonight I was on my own. Not even the

president knew I was here. Sometimes you have to play by your own rules.

On this remote hill in northern Bosnia, near where the concentration camps had been discovered a few years before, I had managed to finally locate a Serb war criminal and part-time terrorist named Vladimir Radovic. He was known to governments around the world and decent people everywhere as Vlad the Bad because of all the innocent people he'd slaughtered when he was in power, before he was on the run.

To me, he was known by a code name, which I thought fit him much better:

The Rat.

I was here to catch the Rat.

Me, Tom Harriman. About to blow past the guns and inside a cabin that had been turned into an armed fortress.

Almost time now. I didn't just feel the darkness all around me, as if night had fallen out of the sky all at once. I could feel another darkness coming up inside me, the way it always did in moments like this, when something was about to happen. When I didn't have to keep my own bad self under control. When I could be one of the good guys but not have to behave like one.

The me that still scares me.

Time to go in and tell the Rat his ride was here.

I should have been cold, as long as I'd been waiting outside. And I knew I should be worried about what might go wrong. Only I wasn't. Cold or worried, take your pick.

As I moved along the front of the tree line, seeing the smoke coming out of the chimney, seeing both levels of the house lit up, I did wonder if it had been too easy finding him. Wondered if the Bads had wanted me to find him, as a way of drawing me here, making me vulnerable.

But that was always part of the fun of it, wasn't it? The finding out.

Someday when Zach is ready, when it is Zach's time and not mine, I will have to tell him the truth about the Bads and about me, tell my kid that the most fantastic story of all was me.

But for now it was time to be the unknown hero again, with the jeep waiting for me on the access road, over on the other side of the woods, with the jet waiting a few miles away in Zagreb. This wasn't the Tom Harriman who testified in front of Congress and briefed the intelligence agencies.

This was the Tom Harriman who did whatever it took to get the job done.

I began to move toward the left side of the house, my

boots not making a sound, even on the frozen snow. One of my many talents, gliding like I was riding an invisible wave.

The front four men were fanned out about fifty yards from the cabin, carrying their rifles like they were looking for any excuse to use them. They didn't know what I knew, that even if they did get to use them, the guns wouldn't do them much good.

And just like that I changed the plan, called an audible on myself, came walking out of the woods, in plain sight, talking to them in their native language.

"I'm lost," I said. "Can you help me out?"

Every gun turned toward me as the guards shouted at me to stop. But I just kept smiling, moving toward them, asking how to find my way back to the main road. I was such a stupid, they probably never met such a stupid in their lives.

The guy in charge just shook his head, turned and said something I couldn't hear, and they laughed, all of them dropping their guns at the same time, like a fighter dropping his hands.

I was on them before they knew it.

It was as if I'd covered the ground between us in one step. Another of my talents. Michael Jordan or LeBron never had a first step like this.

I put all four of them down before any of them could

get his gun back up. Wondered if they could hear the roar inside my head, the one I always heard. It was never adrenaline in times like this, it was something more, something I'd never been able to understand. Or control very well once the bell rang. Most people only see it happen in action movies, one against four, one guy using only his hands and feet for spins and kicks and jumps. Only this was no movie.

It was over quickly, the four of them laid out in the snow, arms splayed like snow angels. Done like dinner, as Zach would say.

It was then that I heard the crackle of the walkie-talkie from inside one of the guards' parkas. Heard a voice full of static, asking Toni why he wouldn't respond, that if he didn't respond right now, he was going to come looking for him.

I didn't know whether the voice was coming from behind the house, one of the four back there that I'd seen earlier, or from someone inside with the Rat.

Someone on the roof trained a huge searchlight on the front yard, making night as bright as day. The first shot was fired then, from somewhere off to my left. Then another. I ducked and rolled and went in a low crouch in the direction of the front door. They were probably wondering how I could still be moving like this, how they'd possibly missed me from close range.

I didn't have time to tell them they probably hadn't missed, that if they were going to put me down, they simply needed bigger guns.

They weren't putting me down and they weren't stopping me. I'd come too far to get the Rat, to take him to the people waiting for him in London, the ones who wanted to either hang him or put him away for the next ten thousand years.

I made it to the porch, the gunfire still crackling all around me.

First floor or second?

He was on the second floor. Don't ask me how I knew; I just did. Call it a sixth sense. So instead of crashing through the door, I jumped up to the second-floor landing.

Don't ask about making a jump like that. You either can or you can't.

I smashed the window and burst through. There he was, the fat slob, trying to make it to the door, turning to fire a shot with the gun in his right hand. But I was across the room before he could do anything, slapping the gun out of his hand, putting my hand behind his neck, finding the spot, putting him out.

I dragged him the rest of the way through the doorway, the two of us in the second-floor hallway. Here came two more of his guys, coming up the stairs with their guns raised but afraid to take the shot because I had pulled the Rat up in front of me, like one of those Kevlar vests you see on the cop shows. I wondered if the vests ever smelled as bad as he did.

It was the stink guys got on them when they were caught.

"Boys," I said to the guys on the stairs, "I'd love to stay and chat, but we've got a plane to catch. And I don't have to tell you what security is like at the airport these days."

"You're not going anywhere," the first one said.

"Well, yeah, actually I am," I said, and kicked him and his friend down the stairs. Then I was over them, flying toward the front door.

I had the Rat under my arm now. I'd played lacrosse in high school, had heard a story once about Jim Brown, who ended up becoming the greatest running back in pro-football history. Brown had been a lacrosse star him-self in high school and later at Syracuse. He was so much bigger, stronger and faster than everyone else that he'd just pin his stick and the ball to his body, run down the field and score, again and again.

They'd had to change the rules so guys like him couldn't do that.

I pinned the Rat to me like that now, backing away from the house as more guys with guns appeared from every angle, all of them afraid to shoot because they might put one in the boss.

I thought about dropping him in the snow so I could go back and finish them all off, because when I got going like this, sometimes I couldn't stop myself.

But we really did have a plane to catch.

So I turned and ran into the woods, not worrying about the hidden trees or branches. I could see in the dark, even without those fancy night-vision goggles the Rat's boys had been wearing. Even with the hard snow pelting my face.

When I got to the other side of the woods, I looked down to the lights of the jeep, making sure that no one was waiting for me there.

It was just when you thought the hard part was over that the real danger began.

Nothing.

I threw the Rat in the backseat and peeled away, hearing the sound of cars starting up behind me. I tore off down the road toward Zagreb, taking the first turn like it was NASCAR.

My ride out of here, a Hawker 4000, was waiting on the runway, which was already covered in snow. I had told the kid who helped run the little terminal for his father that I worked for his president. I didn't tell him why I was here, just told him enough to pull him into tonight's action movie, like the two of us were playing Bond or Bourne.

I'd overpaid the kid by a lot for fuel and maintenance and told him what time I thought I'd be back and told him to have the wings de-iced. If not, the whole mission was a waste of time. Doomed to fail.

His eyes grew wide as plates when he counted the money. Then he nodded and promised me he'd do whatever I needed him to do. I told him that when the plane was in the air to take the money and the jeep he'd loaned me and keep driving until daylight because if he didn't, the guys I'd gone after would be going after him.

I saw two sets of headlights now. They looked to be a couple of minutes behind me, maybe less.

I pulled the jeep up to the plane, untied the Rat, dragged him out of the backseat.

"Him?" the kid said. "It was him you were after?" He crossed himself. Twice.

"Yeah," I said.

"He killed two of my uncles," the kid said. "In the war. Can't you just kill him here and let me watch?"

"Not my brand," I said. "Sorry."

Brand.

Another of Zach's expressions.

The Rat started to wake up. Must be losing my touch, I thought. Usually the claw was good for a few hours.

This time I just slapped him hard, twice, and back out he went.

Headlights from the first jeep appeared at the far end of the runway as I got behind the controls and started taxiing away from them. Soon enough the other jeep came barreling behind.

It was then, in the lights of the Hawker, that I saw a figure walking onto the runway. A man. He wasn't trying to stop me, wasn't carrying a weapon. Wasn't doing anything except standing in the lights, like all he wanted was for me to see him, hair as white as the falling snow showing underneath the old cap he wore down low over his eyes.

What are you doing here? I wondered.

You're supposed to be on the other side of the world.

Not here.

I didn't have time to find out. The plane was already bumping down the runway, shimmying on the ice and snow. And we were airborne, the Rat and me, through the first level of clouds.

Gone.

I tried to focus on flying the plane, getting above the weather, flying until I had to refuel, as I knew I'd have to, between here and London.

But in my mind I kept seeing him on the runway, just standing there.

And that was the problem.

It was never what you thought, never who you thought.

I wanted to feel the rush you felt after you'd won, that feeling the great guys in sports told you they never got tired of. I should have felt great, really, bringing down the Rat, delivering him to people who'd been chasing him a lot longer than I had.

So why did I feel as if I were the one being chased? Even up here, all alone in the night sky?

ZACH Harriman needed to get home.

Not take his time crossing Central Park the way he usually did. Not stop at his favorite bench and read a book the way he sometimes did. Not try to kill a little more time before his dad came home.

Now.

He hadn't slept much the night before. He'd been feeling anxious. He always got this way before his dad came home from one of his "business trips."

Only Zach didn't think of them as regulation business trips. No one did. His dad worked for the government—worked for the president, actually—and Zach would often see him described as a "troubleshooting diplomat" in the newspapers or when he was being introduced on one of the TV news shows.

Zach didn't quite know what his dad did on these trips, but he had a feeling his dad was saving the world one bad place at a time. One time Zach had asked him what it was like, working for the president, and his dad had said in a quiet voice, "I work for the good guys."

He had gone off to Europe this time, some top-secret location Zach and his mom weren't allowed to know.

"That darned national security thing again," his dad had said, almost trying to make a joke of the danger he was probably going to be in.

But it was never a joke to Zach.

People—adults mostly, but kids at school, too—seemed to think every day was like some kind of holiday if you had a famous father. And Zach had to admit, no way around it, that it was a pretty cool deal, being Thomas Harriman's only child.

Except, it was way more cool when he was actually around.

A few months ago, his dad had been in Africa, and the news reports had showed him celebrating with some people he had led back across the border from South Africa into Zimbabwe. At the time, a commentator on CNN had said, "When this country needed him, there he was. Maybe Tom Harriman's real job is hero. And he goes wherever that job takes him."

But, see, that was it right there. That was the problem, to Zach's way of thinking.

The job kept taking his dad. He seemed to belong to the world.

And when you were fourteen, as Zach had just turned, the world that mattered the most to you was your own. Zach Harriman's world was his dad and his mom. It was Alba, Zach's nanny when he was younger, the family's housekeeper and cook now. And it was Kate, the fabulous Kate, Alba's daughter, because she and her mom lived with the Harrimans in their amazing apartment on Fifth Avenue—the top three floors of the great old brownstone Zach's eyes were fixed on now as he crossed the park.

Any kid wanted to have a dad who was brave and respected and famous, no doubt. And a hero, throw that in, too. Yet more than anything, Zach just wanted his dad to be home.

And he would be home tonight, flying his own plane as usual, landing it at Teterboro Airport over in New Jersey. Then he'd head back to the city by car.

Back home, Zach thought.

So Zach should have been happy. Like over-the-moon

happy, not a care in the world. He should have been killing time the way he usually did, because it was still only five o'clock and his dad wasn't scheduled to walk through the front door until seven at the earliest.

Only Zach wasn't happy. He was in a hurry, and a big one.

Starting to run.

And the thing was, he never rushed through the park unless he got caught in some kind of storm and had to beat it home. Other people might think of Central Park, built right in the middle of Manhattan, and think of the trees and green grass, the tennis courts, summer concerts, softball fields, skating rink, more water than most people knew about. And the zoo. And Zach was cool with all that.

But for Zach, Central Park was his own backyard.

The park was a place where he could be alone and not feel alone, where he could run the reservoir or kick a soccer ball around or just wander aimlessly and never be bored. Or stop and watch kids play touch football and pretend that he was in the game with them, that he was just a regular kid.

Sometimes he would walk over to the West Side after school—by himself—and spend an hour at the Museum of Natural History. Go hang with the dinosaurs who used to roam the earth the way his dad did now.

But not today.

Today he was running.

Running like he was being chased. Scared of something without knowing what.

Running hard.

He was close to Fifth Avenue now, could see he was going to make the light, didn't slow down as he crossed the avenue, nearly clipping a nanny he recognized from the neighborhood who was pushing a baby stroller.

He waved and yelled, "Sorry, Veronique!"

Then he slowed down just a little, like his dad downshifting one of his sports cars, as Lenny the doorman opened the front door for him.

"We need to talk about those Knicks," Lenny said.

"Later!" Zach said.

He took a hard right in the lobby, nearly skidding into the wall, heading for the elevator, the one that opened right up into the first floor of the apartment. Knowing the elevator would be waiting for him.

It was.

He took one last look over his shoulder, feeling totally whacked doing it, because he realized what he was doing. Looking to see if the Bads were gaining on him.

The elevator dinged and groaned and began to rise. Zach felt his stomach flip, as though the short ride up was a roller coaster.

The doors opened. Zach walked into the apartment, rounded the corner to the living room. Stopped dead in his tracks.

And he knew.

He knew before he saw all of them. Everyone staring at him with big eyes.

Sad eyes.

The saddest of all belonging to his mom, who clearly had been crying. His mom, who never even wanted anyone to see her crying at the movies.

The whole family was there. Alba. Kate. And John Marshall, the family lawyer, Uncle John to Zach his whole life, even though they weren't actually related.

With them were two policemen, staring at Zach along with everybody else.

Right there and then, Zach knew his dad wasn't coming home tonight. Wasn't coming home, ever.

He'd had it wrong, as it turned out.

The Bads hadn't been chasing him across Central Park after all.

They had been waiting for him here.

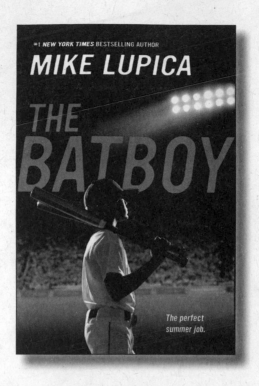

THE BATBOY

Brian is a batboy for his hometown major-league team and believes it's the perfect thing to bring him and his big-leaguer dad closer together. This is also the season that Brian's baseball hero, Hank Bishop, returns to the Tigers for the comeback of a lifetime. But when Hank Bishop starts to show his true colors, Brian learns that sometimes life throws you a curveball.